"Yes," Aidan replied tautly. "I did want to see you. I wanted an explanation as to why you weren't in surgery this afternoon."

Lindsay stared at him. "I went shopping," she replied.

"You went shopping." It was a statement rather than a question. "May I ask if you intend to do that sort of thing on a regular basis? Because if you do, I might as well say here and now that I don't intend continuing as your trainer."

Lindsay felt the blood rush to her cheeks; then, as she turned and shut the door behind her, very briefly she caught sight of the half smile on Bronwen's face. Struggling to control her temper, she strode across Aidan's consulting room and placed her hands on his desk. "Right," she said. "Now that your smug receptionist can no longer hear us, maybe you'll tell me what the hell this is all about."

Dear Reader,

I have been writing fiction since childhood, but it wasn't until my children were growing up and I was working at my local doctor's office that I decided I would like to write a medical romance for Harlequin.

I set my first book on the lovely Isle of Wight, where I was born and raised, and where I still live with my husband. Since that first book eleven years ago, I have gone on to write twenty-eight more medical stories, some set in general practice and others in hospitals.

My inspiration for *Medic on Approval* came from various holidays spent in glorious north Wales, and Snowdonia National Park in particular, which in this story is a contrast to the heroine's former fashionable lifestyle in London. I hope you enjoy reading *Medic on Approval* as much as I enjoyed writing it.

Laura MacDonald
Isle of Wight

# Medic on
# Approval

## Laura MacDonald

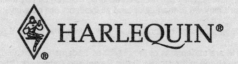

TORONTO • NEW YORK • LONDON
AMSTERDAM • PARIS • SYDNEY • HAMBURG
STOCKHOLM • ATHENS • TOKYO • MILAN • MADRID
PRAGUE • WARSAW • BUDAPEST • AUCKLAND

ISBN 0-373-06309-1

MEDIC ON APPROVAL

First North American Publication 2001

Copyright © 2001 by Laura MacDonald

Visit us at www.eHarlequin.com

**Printed in U.S.A.**

# CHAPTER ONE

'LINDSAY, darling, where is this God-forsaken place that you're going to?' Romilly Souter, Lindsay's father's long-term girlfriend, a little the worse for all the wine she'd consumed during dinner, surveyed Lindsay across the table through half-closed eyes.

'You make it sound as if it's the other side of the world,' Lindsay replied, trying to keep her voice light in spite of a rising sense of irritation. 'It's only North Wales for heaven's sake.'

'But surely that *is* the other side of the world,' said her friend Annabelle Crichton-Stuart from further down the table. 'I remember Daddy taking Rupert and me to Caenarvon once when we were children and us thinking we were never going to get there. It was just mile after mile of mountains and sheep—*and* it rained all the time. It was absolutely ghastly.'

'Oh, I don't know.' This was from Annabelle's husband, Gideon. 'I went to Snowdon once on an Outward Bound course—that was first rate.'

'So tell us, Lindsay, why Wales?' Charles Croad, who was one of her father's oldest friends, leaned forward so that he could see Lindsay.

'Why not?' Lindsay shrugged, still outwardly calm but inwardly beginning to seethe as the opinions she'd feared every since making her decision all began to surface.

'Well…' Charles turned his head to look at Lindsay's father, Richard Henderson, who sat at the

5

head of the table. 'I would have thought something closer to home might have been more sensible. Couldn't you have found her a nice little corner in Harley Street, Richard?'

'Don't you think I've tried?' Richard Henderson gave a short laugh. 'It's Lindsay herself who's insisting on going further afield.'

'But *Wales*,' protested Annabelle. 'Why Wales? It's all rugby and singing and coal mines.'

'Ah, now, there I have to confess.' Richard nodded, his features thrown into sudden harsh relief as the candles on the table suddenly flickered. 'Wales does have something to do with me.' He paused as all chatter around the table died away and ten pairs of eyes turned in his direction. Only Lindsay kept her eyes downcast as she drew patterns in the white damask tablecloth with her thumbnail. 'An old friend of mine, Henry Llewellyn, who also happens to be Lindsay's godfather, has a practice there just outside Betws-y-coed,' Richard continued. 'When Lindsay made up her mind that she wanted to go into general practice I contacted Henry to see if he would take her as a trainee.'

'But I thought Lindsay was a doctor already,' Annabelle interrupted. 'Why would she have to be a trainee?'

'She *is* a doctor,' Richard replied. 'But if she wants to be a GP she needs to do a year's work within a practice to gain experience.'

'Presumably, after that you'll come back to London and to civilisation?' Romilly raised her eyebrows at Lindsay.

'Maybe.' Lindsay looked up quickly.

'Oh, Linds, surely you wouldn't stay there?' wailed Annabelle. 'As it is, you're going to miss absolutely everything this year. Daddy was going to take the boat down to Cowes... Then there was the trip to the villa. Now...' She trailed off with a helpless shrug as Charles Croad spoke again.

'Why general practice, Lindsay? I quite expected you to follow your father into surgery.'

'We all did,' Richard replied. Then, with a wry smile, he added, 'And that's probably the reason.'

Even Lindsay joined in the general laughter that rippled round the table. Her fiercely independent nature was well known amongst her family and friends. Then, as silence fell again, she spoke. 'I want to work with people,' she said quietly.

'You'd do that in Harley Street,' said Romilly with a little sniff.

Lindsay shook her head. 'I don't mean privileged people, I mean ordinary people. People who've had it tough, not people who've had it all handed to them on a plate. I shall work this year in Wales in a rural community with farming people who've had a very difficult time in recent years. After that I shall probably come back to civilisation, as you put it, but if I do it won't be to Harley Street—sorry, Daddy—but to some inner-city area that has social problems.'

'People with social problems also need surgeons,' Richard observed quietly.

'I know that, Daddy,' Lindsay replied, 'just as I know that you're disappointed that I'm not following you into surgery. One day it may happen. I don't know. But at the moment I see my future in general practice.'

There followed a silence around the table which could have become uncomfortable, but then murmuring began afresh as first one and then another topic of conversation was introduced. To Lindsay's relief, the moment passed and she was left in peace.

It was not to be thus for long, however, for later as they lingered over coffee in the drawing room of Richard's beautiful Chelsea home Annabelle once again launched an attack. This time, mercifully, it went unheard by the rest of the gathering and remained simply between the two of them.

'I really will miss you, Linds,' she said accusingly, her rather prominent blue eyes brimming with misery.

'I know, Belle,' Lindsay replied gently. 'And I shall miss you, too. But it isn't for long. A year will pass awfully quickly and I'll be back before you know it. And let's face it, North Wales isn't that far away—you and Gideon could even pay me a visit.'

'Yes, I suppose...' Annabelle replied doubtfully. 'But I thought a while ago when we spoke you said you were postponing this year of training.' Annabelle was sitting on the hearth rug to one side of the fireplace, with her feet tucked under her. As she spoke she glanced up curiously at Lindsay who was perched on the edge of the chesterfield.

'That was then,' Lindsay shrugged but she didn't allow her gaze to meet that of her friend.

'Did that have anything to do with Andrew?'

'Andrew?' she replied lightly. 'It might have done. Why?'

'No reason. I just wondered, that's all.' Annabelle turned her head and stared into the glowing embers of the fire.

There was a long silence then Annabelle spoke again. 'You are over him, aren't you, Lindsay?'

'Of course I am.' Her reply was swift, maybe a little too swift.

'Oh, well, that's all right, then.' She paused. 'Lindsay?'

'Mmm?' It had been her turn to gaze into the fire but she looked up, steeling herself to meet Annabelle's questioning look.

'You will meet someone else, you know.'

'What makes you think I want to?' She raised her dark eyebrows.

'You do. Of course you do. And it'll be different the next time. You just wait. Why, who knows? You might just meet someone in Wales. You know, some rugged sheep farmer or something.'

'Heaven forbid!' Rolling her eyes, Lindsay stood up and turned as her father made his way across the room to join them. 'That's the last thing I want, I can assure you.'

'Well,' said Annabelle, 'I would say it's just what you need.'

Lindsay decided to drive to North Wales even though her father tried to dissuade her.

'I need to take a fair amount with me,' she said, 'and, besides, I shall probably need a car at the practice.'

'You may need something a bit more sturdy on those mountain roads than that sporty little number you drive,' her father replied drily.

'I'll worry about that as and when. I certainly don't intend leaving it behind.' Her sports car had been a present from her father when she'd qualified and quite simply was her pride and joy.

It was a beautiful, clear May morning when Lindsay eventually left her Fulham flat which she'd leased out for the coming year. Her friends had arranged a fare-well party for her on the weekend prior to her departure, and her colleagues at the hospital where she'd been employed as a senior house officer had thrown another party at a local wine bar. It had been one round of goodbyes and such a flurry of activity that Lindsay was almost not sorry to finally be on her way.

She'd planned her route carefully, and instead of all motorway travel had opted instead to head for Oxford, followed by a gentle drive through the Cotswolds into Gloucester, before driving north into Shrewsbury.

The Cotswolds with their buildings of soft, mellow stone and acres of rich, green pasture were quite glorious in the first flush of early summer, and Lindsay felt her spirits lift with every passing mile. This was what she needed, she told herself firmly, to get right away from everything.

What she'd told the guests around her father's dinner table had been quite true—she did want to get out and work with ordinary people, to get away from the privileged lifestyle that she'd been used to all her life—but the urgent need to get away had also arisen since her break-up with Andrew Barlow.

With Andrew she'd thought she'd met the man of her dreams and, at least for her, it had almost been a case of love at first sight. They'd met at a party at the house of a mutual friend in Kensington, and she'd immediately been captivated by the charm and wit of the handsome young solicitor. Their relationship had deepened rapidly, so rapidly that within a couple of months they'd moved in together. At first Lindsay had been blissfully happy. It had only been later, and gradually, that she'd realised that Andrew's charm hadn't been reserved for her alone.

It still hurt even to think about it, and as she pulled

into a service area just outside Worcester once again Lindsay tried to put Andrew right out of her mind.

By the time she reached Shrewsbury her spirits were starting to flag a little, but the roads were good and she pressed on to Oswestry and into Wales, heading for Llangollen. The landscape grew wilder and more dramatic the further north-west she travelled until, at last, the mountains of Snowdonia rose out of the haze, forming a magnificent backdrop as the road wound its way through deep wooded valleys. Mountain streams cascaded from high crevices, crashing down over enormous boulders before gurgling their way over the smooth stones of some ancient river bed. Sheep grazed on every hillside amongst the ferns and heather, sometimes sprawling across the road itself and making driving hazardous.

Just when weariness was threatening to get the better of her and she was beginning to think she would never get there, remembering with a wry smile Annabelle's experience of childhood holidays in Wales, she saw signs for Betws-y-coed and knew that her journey's end was at last in sight. Even then it took her a further hour after a couple of wrong turnings to find the village of Tregadfan, where Henry Llewellyn had his practice.

At least, she thought, the village looked more substantial than some of the others she'd driven through, more like a small town really. For a start there were many more houses while the main street boasted at least two pubs and several shops, and there were signs pointing the way to a tourist centre and caravan park—but of a medical centre there was no sign. At the far end of the village the road took a sudden sharp right-hand bend over a quaint stone bridge.

Lindsay drew off the road and pulled up outside

what appeared to be a little huddle of gift shops. Stiffly she climbed out of the car. There were very few people about, just an old man with his dog and two schoolgirls running down the road, swinging their schoolbags. A quick look at the shops revealed them to be craft shops, all of which were closed. With a sigh she paused for a moment and looked around her.

Deeply wooded pine slopes surrounded most of the village, with the mountains of Snowdonia soaring behind. The beauty of the place was breathtaking, and in spite of her tiredness Lindsay's spirits soared once more. It would be very little hardship to be living and working in such a place for the next year, supposing, of course, she could actually find the place where she was to be living and working. Taking a deep breath, she turned and began to walk back over the narrow stone bridge, pausing for a moment on the parapet to gaze down at the crystal clear water.

On looking up again, she realised that on the far side of the bridge, next to a pub called the Red Dragon, was a small general store. Surely someone in there would know where the local doctor lived.

Three cars were parked outside the shop, together with a mud-spattered Land Rover. Two dogs were sitting in the Land Rover—a Border collie and an Old English sheepdog. The collie barked as Lindsay passed close to the vehicle while a low growl came from the other dog. Lindsay felt relieved that the door of the Land Rover was tightly shut as it looked feasible that the dogs could be quite aggressive in the right circumstances.

A bell sounded loudly as Lindsay pushed open the shop door, surprising her for it was unusual for shops to have bells these days, even remote village shops.

Inside, the layout was that of a small serve-yourself mini-market but, in retaining the best of both ancient and modern traditions, it also boasted a main counter at the far end. Several people were clustered around the counter amid a hum of conversation, but almost before the sound of the doorbell had died away they'd all turned to stare at the newcomer, and as Lindsay advanced towards the counter all conversation ceased.

A man and a woman stood behind the counter, both small in stature, the man with a leathery, ruddy complexion and thinning grey hair and the woman red-cheeked and plump with a bright, bird-like expression. Lindsay hardly noticed the other people around the counter except that, apart from one teenage girl with long dark hair, they all appeared to be men. Some were leaning against the counter while at least two were seated on the type of wooden chairs which once were always seen in shops but which had become a rarity in recent times.

The woman was the first to speak, obviously a question directed at Lindsay but in a language which Lindsay assumed to be Welsh. Her heart sank. What if they all spoke only Welsh? Whatever would she do? How would she communicate with her patients? Taking a deep breath, and only too aware that she was still the object of much suspicious curiosity, she said, 'I'm sorry, but I don't speak Welsh. Do any of you speak English?'

As she spoke she glanced round with what she hoped was a friendly smile at the assembled group. She was met with blank stares and her heart sank even further. One of the men she especially noticed, for his eyes were a startling blue, making his stare seem even sharper than the others. He was leaning against the

counter and was young, probably in his thirties. He had
dark, reddish-brown hair that curled tightly to his head.
He was of only medium height but his body looked
thickset and powerful and, together with his clothing
of jeans, checked shirt and a scruffy waxed jacket, led
Lindsay to assume that he was, no doubt, the farmer
who owned the Land Rover and the dogs.

'What is it you want?' the woman behind the counter
asked. This time she spoke in English, albeit with a
strong Welsh lilt. With a little jolt Lindsay dragged her
gaze away from the man's stare which, because of a
slight air of hostility, suggested his manner could be
as aggressive as that of his dogs.

'Oh,' said Lindsay. 'You do speak English. I'm so
glad. I don't want to buy anything…'

'Oh, aye,' said the woman, her face still expressionless. 'So what do you want, then?'

'I was hoping you could help me.' She paused but
the silence from those around her was almost deafen-
ing. 'I'm looking for a house. It's where Dr Llewellyn
lives. Dr Henry Llewellyn. It's called—'

'So it's the doctor you're looking for, then?' This
interruption was from the man behind the counter.
There was still a look of suspicion on his face but
Lindsay smiled, trying to ignore it.

'That's right,' she said.

The woman continued to eye her up and down, taking in every detail of her appearance from her smart
black trouser suit with its faint pinstripe, which she
wore with a wheat-coloured silk shirt, to her dark hair
tied back with a chiffon scarf, her gold earrings and
wristwatch, and the tan which still lingered after her
recent holiday. 'And where have you come from,
then?'

For one moment Lindsay was tempted to tell the woman it was none of her business where she came from, but she swallowed the retort, putting the woman's apparent nosiness down to natural curiosity. There couldn't be many people, apart from tourists, who arrived in the village, looking for the local doctor. 'I'm from London,' she replied.

After she'd spoken she was aware of some change in the atmosphere amongst those around the counter. It was, however, so slight as to be almost imperceptible, and she found herself wondering if she'd imagined it.

'Oh, from London, are you?' The woman made it sound as if London were on the other side of the world. 'So what would you be wanting with Dr Llewellyn, then?'

She was about to tell the woman that it really wasn't anyone's business but her own, but before she could do so the farmer pushed himself away from the counter, said something in Welsh to the couple behind the counter and sauntered down the shop to the door.

Lindsay watched him go, aware that what he'd said had caused some reaction from the others. Not exactly amusement—that would be hard to imagine from so dour a group—but a general lightening of the atmosphere which, she suspected, was at her expense.

Then, to her relief, the man behind the counter began giving her the directions she needed.

Moments later she left the shop and began to walk back over the bridge. By this time it was early evening. The shadows were beginning to lengthen and a light mist was forming around the mountains behind the village. On the far side of the bridge was a wooden seat, and on a sudden impulse Lindsay decided to phone her father. No doubt he would be fretting and wondering if she'd arrived safely. Sitting down, she took her mobile phone from her bag and dialled her father's number. He answered the phone almost immediately, confirming her suspicions.

'Where are you, Lindsay?' he asked anxiously, after they'd greeted each other. 'Have you got there yet?'

'Yes, that's what I'm ringing for. I'm in the village and I'm on my mobile.'

'Doesn't Henry have a phone at the house? I know he lives in the wilds but isn't that rather taking things to the extreme?'

'I don't know.' She laughed. 'I haven't got to the house yet. I couldn't find it so I went into the village shop to ask the way. I think the locals thought I was something from outer space the way they stared at me—but at least I now know where Henry's house is. I just thought I'd ring you first in case you were sitting there, worrying.'

'Well, no, not really...'

'Come on, Daddy, you know that's not true.'

'Oh, well, all right, then, I suppose I was getting a bit concerned. But you're there now.'

'I'll ring you again, probably tomorrow.'

They said goodbye and Lindsay put her phone back into her bag, stood up and walked back to her car. Two small boys were sitting on the wall, staring admiringly at the car. Lindsay smiled at them and operated the remote control that activated the locks.

'That your car?' asked one of the boys. He had such an accent that Lindsay guessed at what he'd said rather than understood it.

'Yes, it is.' She nodded and smiled again.

'It's dead cool,' said the other boy. 'Like the colour, too. Does it go fast?'

'Fast enough,' Lindsay replied as she slipped into the driving seat. Still the object of the boys' open admiration, she waved a hand and drove away.

According to the man in the shop, Dr Llewellyn's house was outside the village. The practice was behind the chapel, but it would be closed now, she'd been informed, and Dr Llewellyn would be at home. Following the directions, she drove back through the village the way she'd come then took a left turn onto a fairly narrow road.

Lindsay had only travelled a short distance when she saw that there was an obstruction blocking the road ahead. With a muttered exclamation she slowed down and stopped.

There was a large van immediately ahead of her which all but blocked the road, but the problem seemed to be with something that was beyond the van, something outside Lindsay's vision.

She sat for a few moments, tapping the steering-wheel impatiently with her hands. Now she was so close to her destination all she really wanted to do was to get there, have a bath, a meal and a rest. Since she'd stopped in the village her weariness seemed to have caught up with her.

After five minutes or so, when there seemed to be no sign of the problem, whatever it was, resolving itself, Lindsay switched off the engine and climbed out of her car. There was nothing else on the road behind her so she walked forward to the van. It was only then that she realised that the driver wasn't in his cab. Peering round the van, Lindsay could now see that there had, in fact, been an accident a little further up the road. A caravan was on its side, half on the grass

verge and half on the road, and a little group of people
was clustered around someone lying on the ground.

Lindsay started forward, her first instinct to see if
she could help, at the same time silently cursing herself
for sitting in her car, wasting what could turn out to
be valuable time. A young man in blue overalls, presumably the driver of the van, was running towards her.

'What's happened?' she asked.

'Caravan tried to take the corner too fast—he came
out of it.'

'How many are hurt?'

'Two. The old chap has hit his head and his wife
has hurt her arm.'

'I'll see if I can help,' said Lindsay.

'Oh, it's OK,' the van driver replied. 'Ambulance is
on its way—I need to move the van so it can get
through.'

'Even so, some first aid might help.' Not waiting to
hear any more, Lindsay darted forward. She was
vaguely aware that there were other vehicles on the
road beyond the caravan but she didn't take too much
notice of what they were, her main concern being for
the person lying on the ground.

'Let me through,' she said to the people standing
around. 'Please, stand back there and let me through.
I'm a doctor.'

The people did move at that, albeit reluctantly,
Lindsay thought, and as they parted she saw that a
woman was sitting on the grass verge, holding her arm,
and that the person lying on the ground was an elderly
man. Crouching beside him was another man, a man
whose waxed jacket and jeans looked uncomfortably
familiar. As Lindsay stopped he looked up at her over

his shoulder.

Her heart sank as she recognised him. There was no mistaking the owner of that blue-eyed stare. It was the surly farmer who had been in the village shop. 'Oh,' she said abruptly, 'it's you.'

# CHAPTER TWO

'YES,' he said, 'it's me.'

'Can I be of any help?' Lindsay asked, coolly and professionally, she hoped.

'I don't think so.' He stood up. 'I think everything is under control, I doubt if anyone can do any more before the ambulance gets here.'

'I might be able to.' Lindsay crouched down beside the man, who by now was sitting up and holding his head.

'You think so?'

'Well, I *am* a doctor,' Lindsay said tightly, stung by the faint sarcasm in his voice.

'Is that so? Well, in that case, maybe there is something more you can do. Be my guest.' He gestured towards the man on the ground then to the woman sitting on the grass verge.

Ignoring him, Lindsay turned her attentions to the man, who was moaning softly and shaking his head in bewilderment. 'Do you have any injuries anywhere?' she asked, allowing her professional gaze to wander over him. He didn't answer, just shook his head, but there didn't appear to be any sign of bleeding so Lindsay stood up again and hurried across to the woman.

'Is he all right?' the woman asked, peering anxiously across at her husband.

'He appears to be,' Lindsay replied. 'Probably just some concussion. What about you?'

'Just my arm really,' the woman replied, wincing with pain. At that point Lindsay noticed that the woman's wrist was supported inside a scarf which she wore knotted around her neck. 'The man over there said it was broken,' said the woman. 'He put it like this. Said to keep it like this until I get to the hospital.'

'Did he, now?' Lindsay suddenly felt annoyed, but before she could say anything further there came the sound of a siren in the distance. 'Sounds like the ambulance now,' she said, gently touching the woman's shoulder.

'Miss!' There came a shout and Lindsay looked up sharply. The van driver was running down the road, waving his arms. 'The ambulance can't get through. Could you move your car, please?'

Lindsay straightened up. 'Of course,' she muttered.

'Looks like you can be of some use after all,' said the farmer as she hurried past him.

As she reversed her car into a lay-by, Lindsay found she was quietly fuming. There had been something about the man she hadn't liked when they'd met in the village shop, and now she liked him even less. Not simply because he'd known enough to administer first aid—after all, she should have been glad of that—but because of his attitude towards her, especially when he'd found out she was a doctor.

She could see little of what was going on, stuck in the lay-by behind the van, but the arrival of the ambulance was followed by a police Range Rover. While the two patients were taken away to hospital, the police, assisted once more by the farmer in his Land Rover, whom everyone seemed to know, proceeded to move the caravan so that the road was clear once more. At last Lindsay was able to follow the van, and as she passed the group of men standing around the vehicles the farmer nodded to her in acknowledgement.

Somehow Lindsay managed a very cool little nod of her own head in response and then, to her utmost relief, she was finally away, leaving the scene of the incident behind her. A single glance in her driving mirror revealed the farmer, his dogs beside him as he stood in the road, watching her drive away.

Insufferable man, she thought. Hopefully I won't need to see too much of him during my stay in Tregadfan.

Henry Llewellyn's house turned out to be surprisingly close to the scene of the accident, little more than a mile on down the road. Built of stone under a slate roof, it was almost entirely obscured from view by high banks of purple rhododendrons, but as Lindsay drew up before it on the gravel drive it seemed to glow in welcome as it basked in the last of the day's sunshine.

Almost before Lindsay was out of the car the front door was flung wide and a couple of springer spaniels had hurtled forth and were sniffing at her heels.

'Lindsay! How lovely to see you again!' And Henry Llewellyn was there, his arms open wide to greet her, looking exactly as she remembered him from the last time she'd seen him all those years ago when she'd been a student and he'd come to London with his wife, Megan, to visit them.

'Henry! How are you? You haven't changed a bit!'

'The hair and beard's a bit greyer,' he said with a laugh, 'and I dare say there's a bit more midriff than there used to be.'

'Well, you don't look any different to me,' said Lindsay firmly, returning his embrace before turning to open the boot of her car.

'You've changed, though,' he said, standing back. 'Let me look at you. Yes, you were little more than a child before—now I see a beautiful, self-assured young woman. Tell me,' he went on, taking her bags from her as she lifted them from the boot, 'did you have a good journey?'

'Yes, pretty good.' She nodded. 'But it took longer than I thought.'

'You must be tired,' he said over his shoulder as, with the spaniels at his heels, he led the way into the house.

'Yes, I guess I am.' She paused, and as he put her bags down in the hall she said, 'How's Megan?'

'She's…er…resting,' Henry replied, and Lindsay noticed that as he spoke his gaze flickered to the stairs behind her. This didn't sound like Megan, who Lindsay's father had often described as the most energetic woman he knew, and she frowned. Before she could enquire further, however, Henry led the way from the hall into the kitchen. 'Come and have a cup of tea before I show you to your room,' he said. 'Then we can catch up with all the news.'

The kitchen was warm and cosy with evidence of Megan's touch everywhere, from the bunches of dried flowers and herbs hanging from the beam across the Aga to the brightly coloured cushions tied to the seats of the wheel-backed chairs around the central table. Lindsay sat down and watched Henry as he brewed the tea. He enquired after her father and asked if he and Romilly had any plans to marry.

'I don't think so.' Lindsay shook her head. 'They both seem happy with the relationship the way it is. Romilly is a very independent lady and, of course, has her own business.'

'Interior design, isn't it?' asked Henry as he took two mugs down from a cupboard. When Lindsay nodded in response, he went on, 'Megan admires her work.'

'Is Megan working at the moment? Any commissions?' Megan was an artist and ran her own arts and crafts centre in Tregadfan.

When Henry didn't immediately answer, instead standing before the Aga with his back to her, she threw him a curious glance. 'Megan is all right, isn't she, Henry?' she asked tentatively at last.

He took a long time to answer but at last he turned. Carrying the two mugs of tea to the table, he passed one to Lindsay then with a sigh set his own down and sat opposite her. 'No, Lindsay,' he said at last, 'I'm afraid she isn't all right.'

'Oh, Henry.' She stared at him in concern. 'What is it? Whatever is the matter?'

'We're not absolutely sure yet. She's not at all well, but no one is really certain exactly what's wrong. She's had all the usual tests and she's had a scan, which mercifully was negative—but as yet nothing else is conclusive.'

'Do you have any theories?' Lindsay took a sip of tea then set her mug down. It was quiet in the kitchen—even the dogs had settled down in their baskets in front of the Aga and were snoozing with their heads on their paws.

He considered for a long moment then said slowly, 'She had a bout of flu before Christmas—it hit her especially hard and I don't think she entirely recovered from it. She's tired all the time—and I don't mean simply weary, I mean tired—bone tired, so much so that she wants to sleep most of the time. When she's

awake she has constant pain in her joints and muscles.
She's tested negative for multiple sclerosis and for
rheumatoid arthritis…but…' He trailed off, shaking his
head.

'You're thinking ME?' asked Lindsay, reading
Henry's thoughts.

'I'm not sure what else *to* think,' he replied. 'Everything points to that but it's so frustrating, not knowing
for sure. All I do know is that Megan is but a pale
shadow of the woman she was.'

'It must be very difficult.'

'Let's just say it hasn't exactly been easy.'

'What about the family? Are they able to help?'

'Well obviously they've been a great support but
they're all a bit too far away to be of any practical
help. I have a lady who comes in each day to do the
housework…' He looked around him then gave a helpless little shrug.

'And now you've got me to contend with as well.
Honestly, Henry, I would have thought the last thing
you need is a trainee at the present time. Why ever
didn't you tell my father when he contacted you that
it simply wasn't convenient to have me here at the
moment?'

'Oh, Lindsay…' Henry Llewellyn wearily ran a hand
through his hair. 'That's the last thing I would have
wanted to do. Your dad and I go back a long way…'

'I know, Henry. I know,' said Lindsay gently, 'but
it sounds as if you've more than enough to contend
with at the moment without the added responsibility of
a trainee and a house guest into the bargain. I really
don't think I should stay…' She trailed off uncertainly.

'Well, actually, there is an alternative.' Henry threw

her an uncertain glance. 'But I wasn't certain how you would take to the idea.'

'What's that?'

'Well, I tentatively put the idea to my partner that he could take over as your trainer—at least while Megan is feeling the way she is. Maybe if in a little while she beats this thing...' Henry shrugged but his expression showed his doubt.

'And what did your partner say?'

'Well, he'll help out. Of course he will. He's a decent sort of a fellow. Bit of a loner...but nice enough when you get to know him.'

'Who is he?' asked Lindsay curiously. 'I don't think I've heard about your present partner. I only heard Dad talk about old Dr Meredith before he died.' She tried to sound bright, interested even, but inwardly her heart had sunk. One of the reasons for coming all this way to North Wales was because Henry Llewellyn—a man she'd admired since her childhood—was to have been her trainer.

'This one is a young fellow by the name of Aidan Lennox. He's been with me for three years now and he's very good. He's coming in later this evening to meet you.'

'Is there anywhere else I could stay, Henry?'

'Oh, I'm sure that won't be necessary, Lindsay. Megan really wouldn't want that.'

'From what you've told me, Megan really isn't in any condition to have the worry of a house guest at the moment. Surely there must be somewhere else. Maybe I could rent somewhere...'

'That would be easier said than done, what with the tourist season coming up.'

'I thought how quiet it seemed when I was in the village.'

'You just wait until the bank holiday weekend.'

'There must be somewhere…'

'Well, I suppose there's the flat over the surgery,' said Henry doubtfully. 'Aidan stayed there when he first came here before he got his own place. It's empty now.'

'But won't you want to be renting that out during the season?'

'No, we never do that. It wouldn't do to have strangers living in such close proximity to the surgery. The flat is only there because it was part of the house that we bought for the surgery.'

'It sounds ideal,' Lindsay replied. 'Could solve a few problems.'

'Why not wait and speak to Aidan first?' Henry still looked unhappy as if these new arrangements weren't what he'd originally intended at all. 'But whatever happens, you'll be here for the time being. When you've finished your tea I'll take you up to your room.'

The bedroom which had been prepared for her was pretty in a chintzy sort of way but with an oriental theme with prints of Japanese geishas and pagodas. The window overlooked a corner of the garden with a glimpse of the mountains to one side. It was a pleasant room but Lindsay couldn't help but wonder if the new arrangement might not prove to be better in the long term.

The one aspect of the whole venture which had bothered her slightly had been that she was to live with the Llewellyns as their house guest for the duration of her stay. Much as she liked them, she'd seen very little of them in the past and she feared that such conditions might not only put a strain on relationships but at the same time would infringe on her own privacy. Since moving out of her father's house in Chelsea and into her Fulham flat, she'd enjoyed a measure of independence and freedom she wouldn't have dreamed possible.

After she'd showered, changed and unpacked, she decided to go downstairs and see if she could help Henry prepare the meal. She had no sooner stepped onto the landing, however, than she met Henry coming out of another bedroom.

'Ah, Lindsay,' he said as he caught sight of her, 'Megan's awake now. She won't, unfortunately, be joining us for dinner but she'd like to see you.' He held the door open behind him. 'Megan, darling—here's Lindsay now.'

Lindsay wasn't sure quite what she'd been expecting—all she knew was a sense of shock as she saw the woman lying on the bed. The last time she'd seen Megan Llewellyn, which admittedly had been several years ago, had left her the image she carried in her mind. She'd been a vivacious woman—attractive, with dark hair, large expressive eyes and boundless energy. The woman before her bore little resemblance to that image. The most apparent difference was the amount of weight she'd lost. Although never fat, or even plump, Megan had been what Lindsay's father would have termed as well rounded. Now she appeared thin and gaunt, the dark hair greying and the eyes without their lustre. Only her smile was a semblance of what it had once been.

'Lindsay. How lovely to see you again.' She stretched up to receive the kiss Lindsay placed on her cheek. She smelt of some light floral scent as fragile as herself.

'Megan. It's good to see you as well. But I'm sorry to find you feeling so poorly.'

'I wish I'd been able to greet you properly,' Megan replied, and there was no mistaking the wistful sadness in her voice, as if not being able to greet Lindsay wasn't the only thing she regretted not being able to do.

'I'll leave you girls to chat for a while,' said Henry from the doorway. 'I'll go down and get on with the dinner. Will you try a little meat tonight, Megan?'

'I don't think so. I'll just have the soup.'

'Don't you have much appetite?' asked Lindsay, taking a seat beside the bed as, without another word, Henry left the room.

'None at all.' Megan shook her head and it was almost as if the effort of that was too much for her. Clearly exhausted, she lay back against her pillows. 'It worries Henry sick, I know, but I can't help it. I simply can't eat.'

'Henry tells me this goes back to a bout of flu you had.'

'Yes. Did he tell you they suspect ME? I'd heard of ME but, I have to admit, I was sceptical about it. I know differently now.' Megan sighed. 'It's the tiredness that gets me the most. The slightest effort and I'm absolutely exhausted. Most everyday activities are quite simply out of the question. But...' she faltered slightly '...it's Henry I feel sorry for. It's put so much onto him...'

'You mustn't lose heart, Megan.' Lindsay leaned forward and covered the older woman's hand. 'ME is becoming much more recognised now and I'm sure research will bring up something new very soon by way of treatment.' She stood up and, looking down at Megan who'd closed her eyes, she said, 'I've tired you. I'm going down now to see if I can give Henry a hand. I understand his partner is coming over for dinner. I'll see you later, Megan.'

She doubted Megan even heard her, and as she stole from the room and quietly closed the door behind her her heart went out to the woman whose pale shadow was all that had been there on the bed.

As she hurried down the stairs Lindsay heard the sound of voices and imagined that Henry's partner must have already arrived. But as she approached the kitchen all was silent within, and when she pushed the door open she found that Henry wasn't there. Instead, a man stood with his back to her, looking out of the window to where Henry could be seen outside on the lawn with his dogs.

'Hello,' she said. 'I thought I heard voices. You must be...' But that was as far as she got for at the sound of her voice the man turned, and as she caught sight of his face the words died on her lips. Before her stood the farmer she'd first seen in the village shop and later at the scene of the accident. He looked different now— the checked shirt and jeans had been replaced by a roll-necked cotton shirt and olive green chinos—but there was no mistaking him. The dark, reddish-brown curly hair was the same, the bright blue eyes were the same and the unsmiling countenance was the same.

'Oh,' she said, recovering sufficiently to say, 'I wasn't expecting to see you again today.'

'Really?' Still no smile, just raised eyebrows.

'Are you a friend of Henry Llewellyn?'

'A friend?' He paused. 'Well, I suppose you could

say that, yes. I would say we are friends. Don't always see eye to eye, but friends? Yes.'

Lindsay frowned. If he was a friend of Henry's why the hell hadn't he spoken up in the village shop when she'd been asking the way to his house? She had no time to ponder further for at that moment the back door opened and Henry himself appeared, kicking off his muddy boots and thrusting his feet into a pair of old leather slippers.

'Ah!' he said, catching sight of Lindsay, 'Good, I see you two have met. I gather introductions are unnecessary, then?'

'Actually, I've only just come down,' Lindsay replied.

'Well, in that case…' Henry looked from one to the other '…Aidan, I'd like you to meet Lindsay Henderson. Lindsay, my dear—this is my partner, Aidan Lennox.'

'Y-your p-partner?' stammered Lindsay. 'But… but…I thought…'

She stared at him and from the expression in those penetrating blue eyes she knew immediately that he'd known who she was—had known all along. Desperately she attempted to pull herself together, forcing herself to take his outstretched hand.

'Pleased to meet you at last,' he said, and his voice held a slightly mocking note.

Damn him, she thought. Damn the man. Even if he hadn't come to her rescue in the shop, he could have established the fact at the scene of the accident that he also was a doctor. As it was, he'd allowed her to make a fool of herself in front of him. She wanted to challenge him with it—indeed, opened her mouth to do so—but Henry spoke first.

'I do hope you two are going to get along,' he said, looking from one to the other again, 'especially as you're going to be working so closely.'

It was neither the time nor the place to challenge him. To have done so would have simply been discourteous to Henry, so instead she simply nodded and said, 'Pleased to meet you, too, Dr Lennox.' Inwardly, however, she promised herself that she would confront him with his surly behaviour when the time was right. But a little later, when they went through to the dining room and Henry poured drinks, it gradually dawned on her that if this man had simply been a friend of Henry's it would have been easy to cope with as she would hardly have to see him, but as it was he was her trainer, and they would be in each other's company a great deal. As the full implication set in, her spirits sank even further.

Dinner was a difficult meal, and if Henry was oblivious to an undercurrent both Lindsay and Aidan Lennox were only too aware of it. Conversation centred for a time on Lindsay's life in London, and she could feel Aidan's air of disapproval of the apparent privileges of her lifestyle as if it were some tangible thing.

At the end of the meal Henry leaned back in his chair. 'Lindsay was saying she thought it would be more practical if she was to live elsewhere during her year with us,' he said. 'I suggested the surgery flat—how do you feel about that, Aidan?'

'Makes no difference to me.' Aidan shrugged.

'You found it quite adequate, didn't you, whilst you were there?' Henry persisted.

Aidan nodded. 'Yes, but my tastes are very simple—I doubt the Tregadfan surgery flat measures up to a Chelsea town house.'

Lindsay felt the colour flood her face but, keeping perfectly calm, she replied, 'The Chelsea house is my father's—I have my own flat in Fulham.'

'Just as comfortable, I would imagine?' Aidan raised his eyebrows again in that maddening way he had.

'Oh, I'm sure it is,' Henry replied innocently, totally oblivious to any undercurrent. 'Didn't Richard buy it for you, Lindsay, for your twenty-first birthday?'

'Er, yes,' she admitted reluctantly.

'There can't be too many SHO's living in such luxury,' observed Aidan. 'My own hospital days were a far cry from that. In fact, I'm surprised you've deigned to join us in our humble little corner of the world. I would have thought something in Harley Street would have been more in your line.'

'Actually,' Lindsay retorted, stung into a reply by his tone, 'I was offered Harley Street, but I turned it down.'

'You wanted something in the real world, didn't you, Lindsay?' said Henry with a laugh.

'Well, you'll certainly get that here.' Aidan's retort was cryptic. 'And while we're on the subject, you'll have to do something about that car of yours.'

'My car?' Lindsay looked up sharply. 'What's wrong with my car?'

'There's nothing wrong with your car,' replied Henry hastily. 'In London, that is. I think what Aidan means is that it may not be practical for some of our roads around here.'

'Henry drives a Jeep and I drive a Land Rover,' said Aidan.

'I know,' Lindsay replied coolly. 'I thought you were a farmer instead of a doctor.'

'And what's wrong with being a farmer?' His tone was as cold as his eyes.

'Nothing…'

'There are plenty of them about in this community, and if you're going to stay here you'll have to get used to them.'

'Whoa, wait a minute.' Henry broke in as this rapid exchange of fire looked as if it could be about to escalate into a full-scale spat. 'Have you two met before?' He looked from one to the other in bewilderment.

'Yes,' said Lindsay shortly. 'At least, we've seen each other. In the village shop when I stopped to ask the way…and…'

'Later at a little pile-up further up the road,' Aidan continued smoothly, 'when you rushed to volunteer your professional services.'

'Well!' said Henry, shaking his head. 'Well, I never. You should have said.' He stood up, still looking baffled. 'You'll have to excuse me. I must go up to Megan but I'm sure the two of you will find plenty to talk about.' With that he walked out of the room, shutting the door behind him and, to Lindsay's dismay, leaving her alone with the insufferable Aidan Lennox.

# CHAPTER THREE

THEY sat in silence for a few moments then Lindsay, deciding this was as good a time as any, took a deep breath. 'Why didn't you say who you were?' she asked abruptly.

Aidan appeared to be staring at something through the window behind her as if he were lost in a world of his own and hadn't even heard what she'd said. In growing irritation she was about to repeat the question when he refocused and looked at her. 'What do you mean?' His answer was equally abrupt.

'In the shop,' she went on. 'You must have realised who I was when I asked for directions.'

'Why should I? Tourists are always asking for directions.'

'You thought I was a tourist?' When he gave a slight shrug, she added, 'Do many tourists ask for Henry Llewellyn?'

'Tourists are always asking for doctors.'

'All right. So you may have thought at that point I was just another tourist. But what about afterwards, at the accident, when you heard me say I was a doctor? You must have known then but you said nothing and allowed me to make a fool of myself.'

'Did you?' A faint frown creased his forehead. 'I wasn't aware you'd made a fool of yourself.'

'Those people knew you were a doctor—they didn't need another one at that point. If you'd only said who you were, I would have...'

'Would have what?' he asked coolly.

'Well, I would have... Oh, I don't know, but I certainly wouldn't have gone blundering in where I wasn't wanted.'

'If I remember rightly, you went blundering in, as you put it, before I had the chance even to speak.'

'You still could have said...'

'You were so intent on doing good—'

'But you must have realised then who I was.'

'Yes, I suppose so.' Aidan shrugged and there was little enthusiasm about the gesture.

'So why didn't you say anything then?' Lindsay demanded.

'If I remember rightly, the ambulance arrived and you were asked to move your car.'

She didn't answer. It was true. Everything he'd said was true. So why was she still left with the uncomfortable feeling that he'd known who she was from the beginning and had deliberately avoided revealing his own identity?

'You're here now,' he said at last, 'and, really, all this is irrelevant so we might as well forget it.'

'Maybe.' She nodded. 'But I feel we've got off to a bad start—and for no good reason.'

'And was it important to you that we should have got off to a good start?' he asked smoothly.

Lindsay stared at him, noticing as she did so a small triangular scar on the side of his left cheek. Probably where some exasperated woman had landed him one for being so infuriating, she thought. 'Well, it might have helped,' she replied at last. 'Especially now I've been told that you're to be my trainer.'

'Ah, yes.' Briefly his nostrils flared as he inhaled

sharply. 'And did it bother you when you found that out?'

She took a deep breath. 'Actually, yes, it did if you must know—'

But that was as far as she got for at that moment the door opened and Henry appeared again. 'Sorry about that,' he said.

'Megan all right?' asked Aidan.

'About the same,' Henry replied with a sigh.

'I'll go up and see her before I go.'

Henry must have seen Lindsay's look of surprise. 'Aidan is our GP,' he explained.

'Really?' Lindsay couldn't understand why Henry and Megan should want this exasperating man anywhere near them, especially when they were ill, even if he was Henry's partner.

'I'm sure you two found plenty to talk about,' said Henry as he carried the coffee percolator to the table. 'I've spoken briefly to Lindsay about you taking over as her trainer, Aidan.'

'So I gather.' Aidan nodded.

'I know it isn't what any of us had planned,' Henry went on as he poured the coffee, 'but there was no knowing that Megan was going to be as ill as this.'

'I still think this is an added and unnecessary burden for you at this time, Henry,' said Lindsay as she took the cup and saucer that Henry handed to her. 'And I happen to think the best thing would be for me to go back to London.' Suddenly that prospect had its attractions. Probably anything would be preferable to working with the objectionable Dr Aidan Lennox.

Henry, it seemed, was of a different opinion. 'Nonsense,' he said briskly. 'There's no reason why you shouldn't stay, especially as Aidan has agreed to take you on. Besides, with the way things are here, we could do with another pair of hands.'

'But won't I just be a liability?' Lindsay frowned and at the same time carefully avoided Aidan's eye.

'Not at all. You're only a trainee GP, for heaven's sake,' Henry replied. 'It might have been a different matter if you were a trainee doctor. But you're fully qualified and I can only see that as being an asset to us in our present circumstances.'

'Really?' she said doubtfully. She was only too aware that Aidan had remained absolutely silent and was sitting as still as stone.

'Yes, really,' Henry replied firmly. 'I'm quite limited with what I can do at the moment. It will be such a relief to have someone else around who can share the burden. Take night duty, for instance—there have been times recently when I've been reluctant to leave Megan when I've been on call, but I've had no choice because I could hardly call on Aidan when I knew he'd been up all the previous night. Besides, I can't have you going home, Lindsay. You've given up your job and turned your life upside down to come here for a year. Whatever would your father think?'

'I'm sure he'd understand—'

'No.' Henry stood up and began clearing the table. 'I won't hear another word on the matter. I've already made two concessions in that Aidan will take over as your trainer and that you will live in the flat, and that is as far as I'm prepared to go.'

'Well, if you put it like that...' She trailed off with a helpless little shrug, still avoiding Aidan's eye. 'When would you like me to start?'

'Just as soon as you like.' The relief in Henry's voice was only too apparent. 'I suggest you come down to the surgery with me tomorrow morning and familiarise yourself with the place and then Bronwen can show you the flat.'

'Who's Bronwen?' She did glance up then and was in time to see what could have been the semblance of a smile flit across Aidan's granite-life features.

'Bronwen? Ah, well, Bronwen looks after us all,' said Henry. 'She's sort of head receptionist...office manager—you name it—all rolled into one. Don't know what we'd do without her. Isn't that right, Aidan?''

Aidan nodded. 'She also rules the roost,' he said. 'You upset Bronwen at your peril.'

'You sound as if you speak from experience,' Lindsay remarked drily.

'Oh, Aidan's had a few spats with our Bronwen, especially when he first arrived.' Henry gave his rich chuckle.

Soon after that Lindsay excused herself, pleading tiredness after her long journey, and thankfully went to her room, leaving the two men talking of practice matters.

It was relief to get into bed and finally to relax. It had been a tiring day and at journey's end nothing had really been as she had expected. She wasn't looking forward to the next day, or any other day after that if she was really honest, but it seemed there was little she could do about the situation. Just before she slipped into the welcome mists of sleep she decided that all she could really do was to make the best of things, but at the same time she resolved that she wouldn't let herself be intimidated by Aidan Lennox, by the indomitable Bronwen or by anyone else for that matter in this rather strange village.

*    *    *

Lindsay awoke the following morning to the sound of heavy rain pattering on the roof. For one moment she couldn't think where she was. As she remembered, she gave a groan and, turning over, buried her face in the pillow.

The rain did little to restore her spirits and it was with a heavy heart that she joined Henry in the kitchen.

'Ah, Lindsay, my dear.' His greeting was warm but he looked tired, and Lindsay wondered if Megan had had a bad night. 'I trust you slept well.'

'Like a log. How is Megan this morning?' she added quickly as she helped herself to coffee and toast.

'Not very bright. She had a bad night with muscle pain but she's sleeping now.'

'Are you able to leave her?'

'The daily help will be in shortly—she's very good. She'll get anything Megan wants and I shall pop back at lunchtime.' With that he left Lindsay to eat her breakfast while he took the dogs out for a run. When he returned she heard him on the phone in the hall then a moment later he looked round the kitchen door. 'Well, if you're fit, shall we make a move?' he said.

Lindsay nodded took a last gulp of coffee and followed him out into the hall where she picked up her jacket, her case and her keys.

As Henry quietly closed the front door behind them he said, 'May I suggest you come with me in the Jeep this morning?'

Mindful of Aidan's derision over her sports car, Lindsay pulled a face.

'You mustn't let Aidan bother you,' said Henry a few minutes later as he drove the Jeep out onto the road, with Lindsay beside him, and headed for the village. It was still raining hard and this morning the mountains were shrouded in thick cloud. 'Remember, I told you,' he added, 'it takes a bit of getting to know Aidan, but when you do it's worth the effort because he's all right.'

'I'll bear that in mind,' replied Lindsay drily, 'when he's having a go at me because of my background.'

'You mustn't mind that either,' said Henry. 'It's a bit of a sore point with him—he had a very rough ride in his bid to become a doctor. I gather money was very tight and several times it was touch and go whether or not he would be able to finish his studies.'

'Well, that must have been very tough, I'm sure,' said Lindsay, 'but it's hardly my fault. Neither is it my fault that my father happens to be well off and successful. And at the end of the day none of that made the slightest difference to whether or not I passed my exams—I had to work as hard as anyone else.'

'I'm sure you did,' said Henry soothingly. 'All I'm saying is don't let Aidan get to you.'

And that, thought Lindsay as they took a narrow turning beside the chapel then swung onto the forecourt of a tall stone house, is going to be easier said than done.

A small woman with softly curling brown hair and whose age was difficult to determine, but who could have been anywhere between thirty and forty, was behind the reception desk, sorting through the morning mail. She barely glanced up as Henry and Lindsay shut the front door behind them and approached the desk. Before anyone had a chance to speak, a door opened to the left of them and a girl with long mousy hair and a terrified expression on her face, carrying a tray with three steaming mugs, came out and set the tray down on the desk.

'Oh!' she gasped when she caught sight of Henry.
'Oh, Dr Llewellyn, I didn't know you'd arrived. I'll go
and make some more coffee.' She would have darted
back into the room she'd come from but Henry stopped
her.

'No, wait a moment, Gwynneth,' said Henry. 'I'm
glad you're both here. I would like you to meet Dr
Lindsay Henderson.' Turning, he took Lindsay's arm
and drew her forward. 'Lindsay, my dear, these are the
ladies who keep the place ticking over for us. This is
Gwynneth, who hasn't been with us very long and is
still learning the ropes, and this...' he indicated the
lady behind the desk '...is Bronwen. Bronwen has been
with us for a very long time and knows everything
there is to know about the practice. If there's anything
you want or need to know you only have to ask
Bronwen.'

So, thought Lindsay, this is the formidable Bronwen.
She didn't know quite what she'd been expecting—
probably some Amazon-like woman with warlike ten-
dencies—certainly not the petite figure with the rather
serious expression who gravely inclined her head in
greeting.

Once the formalities were over Henry asked if Dr
Lennox had arrived.

Gwynneth opened her mouth to reply to Henry's
question but Bronwen stepped in smartly, giving the
girl no chance to speak. 'Yes,' she replied crisply, 'he's
been in. But he's gone over to the Dragon to see
Thomas who had a bad night with his emphysema. He
won't be long.'

'Very well. Tell him we'll be in my room when he
gets back. Oh, Bronwen, is Dr Henderson's room ready
for her?'

'Of course.' Bronwen's response was abrupt, as if she was affronted that Henry should even think otherwise.

'Well done, but we'll need to see you, Bronwen— there have been one or two changes to the original plan.'

'Oh?' Bronwen looked up sharply. 'And what might those be?'

'We'll put you in the picture when Dr Lennox gets back.' Henry's tone implied that for the moment, at least, the matter was closed. Lindsay, however, had caught sight not only of Bronwen's expression, hostile now as she anticipated what changes might have been made without her knowledge, but also of Gwynneth's scared one, as if she, too, feared the consequences. Lindsay was thankful to follow Henry out of Reception.

'This is my consulting room,' said Henry, opening the door and revealing a spacious, airy room at the front of the house. 'Aidan's is across the way and yours is down here. Come and have a look.' He led the way down a fairly narrow passage to the rear of the house where he threw open a door. 'This was the breakfast room originally when this was a family home,' he said.

It was a light room even on a bleak rainy morning so Lindsay could imagine it would be really bright and pleasant on a sunny one. There were French doors on one wall which led into a plant-filled conservatory. A large window on another wall looked out over a small but pretty garden surrounded by a dry stone wall and with the inevitable mountain backdrop. A large oak desk bearing a computer stood in front of the window while a curtained-off section of the room revealed an examination couch.

'I hope this will be suitable for you, Lindsay.' There was a decided touch of anxiety in Henry's voice and she hastened to reassure him.

'It's a lovely room,' she replied, then she paused, before saying, 'Do you intend me to take surgeries straight away?'

'More or less, we thought. Although you'll have to talk to Aidan about what he has in mind.'

'What about the flat?' She looked round at her surroundings. 'Can I see that now?'

'Well, I've arranged for Mrs Jones, who's our cleaner, to come in this morning to tidy it up a bit and to give it the once-over—you know, air the place a bit, that sort of thing. I think I'd rather you wait to see it until then.'

'Is this something I should know about?' Unheard by either of them, Bronwen had come into the room behind them and was standing in the doorway.

'Oh, Bronwen, this was one of the changes I was telling you about. Dr Henderson has decided that in view of my wife's illness she won't be staying at the house. She'll probably be staying upstairs in the flat, but I want Mrs Jones to have a go at it before Dr Henderson sees it.'

'Why?' asked Bronwen. 'It's perfectly clean and tidy up there.'

'Oh, I'm sure it is,' replied Henry hastily. 'But, well, I know we've been storing things up there—'

'Only some files,' said Bronwen frostily.

'Yes, well, no doubt the place wants airing.' Henry turned quickly as someone else entered the room. 'Oh, Aidan, there you are. I was just telling Bronwen that Lindsay will probably be living upstairs in the flat while she's with us.'

'I see,' said Aidan, looking round and, no doubt, summing up the atmosphere in the room. Briefly his gaze came to rest on Lindsay and he gave her a cool nod. 'Good morning,' he said. Turning to Henry again, he went on, 'Have you also told Bronwen that you're no longer to be Lindsay's trainer?'

'Er, no, I hadn't quite got around to that,' Henry replied. 'I thought we should wait until you arrived.'

'Well, I'm here now,' said Aidan, 'so I guess there's no time like the present. Bronwen, it's been decided that I am to be Dr Henderson's trainer instead of Dr Llewellyn.'

Lindsay was watching Bronwen to see what her reaction would be to this particular piece of information. She had gathered from the behaviour of the two men that some sort of reaction would be inevitable and, probably because she was anticipating it, she saw the quick look of surprised annoyance that crossed the woman's face. It was gone almost immediately and replaced by her usual rather bland expression.

'When was this decided?' she asked.

'A couple of weeks ago,' said Henry.

'It would have been nice to have been kept informed,' said Bronwen tightly.

'We decided not to say anything until we'd spoken to Dr Henderson,' said Henry. 'I very much regret having to take this decision but in view of Mrs Llewellyn's illness it seemed the only thing to do. Luckily, both Dr Lennox and Dr Henderson have agreed to the change.'

'So how will surgeries be arranged?' Bronwen turned to Aidan.

'That still needs to be discussed.' He glanced questioningly at the other two. 'Is it too early for a confab now?'

'Not at all,' said Henry briskly. 'Come along to my room. Bronwen, maybe you could organise coffee for us all?'

Bronwen murmured something unintelligible and retreated back to Reception while Henry and Aidan looked ruefully at each other. Moments later they all three were seated in Henry's consulting room and Bronwen appeared with a tray bearing three mugs of coffee and milk and sugar, which she set down on Henry's desk.

'Shall I stay?' she asked.

Henry shook his head. 'No, Bronwen, we mustn't keep you from your other duties. It's always busy for you at this time of the morning. But, rest assured, you'll be informed immediately of what we decide.'

With a sniff Bronwen left the room, shutting the door behind her with a loud click.

'Why do you let her do it?' asked Lindsay. She was totally mystified by the interchange with Bronwen.

'Do what?' Aidan helped himself to milk and sugar.

'Rule the roost,' replied Lindsay simply.

'She doesn't really,' said Henry, shaking his head.

'She only thinks she does,' Aidan explained. Once again Lindsay saw that fleeting semblance of a smile as it crossed his features.

'Bronwen is actually very good at her job,' said Henry. 'Good staff are hard to come by here as nearly all the young people leave this area when they finish school to seek work elsewhere. So, yes, I admit, we do tend to humour Bronwen by allowing her to think she actually has more power than she really does.' He paused and sipped his coffee, pulled a face then added sugar. 'Now down to business. Aidan. Before, when we talked, when I was to be Lindsay's trainer, we agreed that it would probably be best if she were to take any extra surgeries—are you still in agreement with that?'

'Yes, I think so.' Aidan nodded then turned to Lindsay. 'It simply isn't feasible for you to have your own list of patients when you're only here for such a relatively short space of time. During the summer months, as you can probably imagine, we become inundated with tourists who never seem to be able to get through a week's holiday without the attention of a doctor. It would be of immense help to us if you were to take those extra surgeries of temporary residents.'

Lindsay frowned. This wasn't quite what she'd expected. 'So am I only to do that?' she asked. 'I can't imagine I'll learn too much about general practice simply by tending to holiday ailments.'

'You'd be surprised,' said Aidan drily.

'There will be more to it than that,' said Henry quickly. 'We also have a surplus most days of our own patients when appointments become hopelessly overbooked. We propose that you see these extra patients as well. We may also require you to make some home visits for us,' he went on. 'There will be times when I may be otherwise engaged, possibly with Megan, and unable to carry out home visits—likewise, if Aidan is having a day off.'

'Will you want me to start this straight away?' asked Lindsay. Suddenly she felt rather alarmed for it sounded as if she was to be flung in at the deep end.

'It's up to Aidan when you start,' said Henry, turning to look at his partner. 'I'm not sure what he has in mind. Aidan?'

'I'll want you to sit in on a few surgeries with me to start with,' Aidan replied, 'because you'll need to get the feel of the place and the people. After that, we'll swap places and I'll sit in on your surgeries for a while. You can accompany both Henry and myself on house visits so that you can get to know the area. What do you think, Henry?'

'Oh, absolutely,' said Henry with a laugh. 'We can't have you getting lost, Lindsay, on some remote mountain pass. Speaking of which, we must organise a suitable vehicle for you to drive while you're here.'

At that moment the intercom sounded on Henry's desk and he flicked the switch. 'Yes, Bronwen?' he said with a sigh.

'You have a lot of patients out here, Dr Llewellyn.' Bronwen's barely veiled accusing tone could be heard quite clearly by all three of them. 'What would you like me to tell them?'

'No need to tell them anything, Bronwen. We're about to start surgery now.'

'And where will Dr Henderson be?'

'Dr Henderson will be sitting in with Dr Lennox,' Henry replied firmly.

The sound of a loud click from the intercom indicated that Bronwen had switched off.

'Well, that's that,' said Henry with a chuckle. 'I guess we'd better get a move on.'

'Yes,' agreed Aidan drily. 'I guess we had.'

# CHAPTER FOUR

AIDAN'S consulting room was on the far side of Reception. As large as Henry's, it looked out over the village and possessed its own examination room. After indicating to Lindsay to take a seat close to his, Aidan spent a few minutes explaining the computer system to her.

'I obviously don't expect you to remember it all at once,' he said.

'It shouldn't be too much of a problem,' she replied airily. 'We had the same system at the hospital where I last worked.'

'That may well be so,' he said, then added ominously, 'But I bet you didn't have a Gwynneth.'

'Gwynneth?'

'Yes, Gwynneth is a dab hand at crashing the system.'

'Oh, I see...' Lindsay trailed off, for at that moment, as if on cue, Gwynneth tapped on the door and came into the room, bearing a bundle of notes in her hands.

'Ah, Gwynneth,' said Aidan calmly, 'we were just talking about you.'

The girl flushed scarlet. 'Oh, were you?' she said, and Lindsay got the impression that, far from being embarrassed, she was pleased she was the object of their attention.

'Yes.' Aidan nodded. 'I was just telling Dr Henderson what a dab hand you are with the computer.'

49

'Oh, well…' Gwynneth flushed even deeper. 'I try my best but I don't always get things right,' she said in her lilting Welsh accent. 'Sometimes I spend ages putting something in then I press one button and it all disappears.'

'Are those this morning's notes, Gwynneth?' asked Aidan.

'What?' said Gwynneth dreamily.

'The notes?'

'Oh, yes. Here you are.' She handed them over. 'I almost forgot what I'd come in for.' Still with a dreamy expression on her face, she left the room.

'As you can see,' said Aidan, 'we sometimes have a bit of a problem with our Gwynneth. But she means well.'

'I'm sure she does,' Lindsay replied.

'Right, if you're ready, we'll get started.'

She watched as he leaned forward and pressed a buzzer, presumably for the first of the morning's patients. This morning he was casually dressed in a navy blue cotton sweater and light beige trousers. It was all very informal, and as Lindsay glanced down at the black suit and crisp white blouse she was wearing she felt decidedly overdressed.

The first patient of the morning was an elderly man who stared suspiciously at Lindsay as soon as he came into the room.

'Ah, Hew, this is Dr Lindsay Henderson. She's going to be joining us here at the practice for a while,' said Aidan.

'She's a doctor, you say?' Hew Griffiths still looked suspicious.

'Yes, she is. She's fully qualified and she comes to us from London.'

'Good morning, Mr Griffiths,' said Lindsay.

'London, you say?' he said, ignoring Lindsay's greeting. 'My old dad used to say nothing good ever came out of London, and that was then, in his day. And from what I've seen lately in the papers, little seems to have changed. Den of vice it is down there.'

'Hardly that, Hew.' Aidan spoke firmly but Lindsay had the feeling he was amused by the old man's observations. 'Now,' he went on, 'what can we do for you?'

'You want me to say now?' Hew Griffiths stared at Lindsay.

'Yes, please.' Aidan nodded.

The old man frowned then, taking a deep breath, he brought forth a torrent of Welsh.

'No, Hew.' Aidan shook his head. 'Not Welsh. English, please.'

With a scowl in Lindsay's direction Hew began to mutter something. As far as Lindsay was concerned, he might as well still have been speaking in Welsh for all she understood.

'So you say you've been passing water more frequently?' said Aidan, coming to her rescue. 'Is this during the day or is it mainly at night?'

Hew nodded. 'Yes, night-time,' he muttered.

'And when you go, Hew, is it a constant stream?'

He shook his head without looking at Lindsay.

'More of a stopping and starting affair? Is that it?'

A nod this time.

'I think I need to take a look at you, Hew. If you'd like to go into the examination room and slip your trousers off.'

In panic the old man threw Lindsay a wild glance.

'It's all right, Hew, it'll only be me,' said Aidan. As

Hew Griffiths took himself off to the examination room Aidan looked at Lindsay. 'You don't mind, do you?' he asked.

She shook her head. 'No,' she said, 'they're bound to be suspicious of me to start with. Just as long as they let me treat them when I'm taking my own surgery.'

'I think by then they'll have come to realise that you're a doctor in your own right. Probably seeing you in here with me, they automatically jump to the conclusion that you're some sort of student.' Aidan stood up and, crossing to the examination room, went inside, shutting the door behind him.

With a sigh Lindsay looked round the room. Not for the first time she found herself wishing she was back in the accident and emergency department of the London hospital she'd recently left. No one there had queried whether she'd been a doctor or not. The fact that she'd been wearing a white coat and had had a stethoscope round her neck had usually been all that had been needed, and patients had just been grateful that it had been their turn at last to be seen. But, she reminded herself sternly, it had been her choice to go into general practice, just as it had been her choice to come here to North Wales to do her training, rather than settling for the more familiar surroundings and situations she was used to. The fact that nothing was working out the way she'd hoped was really nothing she could do much about.

Perhaps she would have to learn to adapt more. For a start she wouldn't drive her expensive and utterly unsuitable sports car round the mountain roads. Maybe she should also look out something different to wear— less Kensington High Street and more mountain village, she told herself wryly as the door opened and Aidan came out of the examination room. Crossing to the sink, he began washing his hands.

Then quite suddenly, as she watched him, Lindsay felt a swift, unreasonable surge of irritation. Why did it have to be her who should change? This wasn't what she'd envisaged at all, having as her trainer a man she didn't even particularly like, so why should it be her who had to do the adapting?

And then she realised Aidan was talking to her. He still had his back to her but he was talking, and because she'd been feeling so annoyed she hadn't heard a word he'd said. While she was still wondering whether she should ask him to repeat himself he looked over his shoulder at her.

'Well?' he asked. 'What would you have done?'

'Er…in Mr Griffiths's situation?' Lindsay said, taking a guess at what he'd asked her.

'Well, yes, who else did you think I meant?'

'I would have needed to examine him first,' she said quickly.

'Quite.' Turning from the sink, he began drying his hands. 'That's why I've just explained my findings to you.'

'Oh,' she said, aware that her face had flushed with embarrassment.

'Would you like me to repeat my findings?' He raised his eyebrows.

'Yes, please,' she mumbled.

'Enlarged prostate,' he said briefly.

He was obviously waiting now for her contribution but there was something about the directness of his stare that Lindsay found very disconcerting. In the end she had to make a conscious effort to pull herself together, while at the same time inwardly cursing herself for her lapse of concentration. 'I would say blood tests then a referral to a consultant for further investigation,' she said at last.

At that moment Hew Griffiths reappeared so Aidan merely nodded in agreement with her before sitting down at his desk again.

'I'm going to get you an appointment, Hew, to see a specialist,' he told the patient.

'Eh?' Hew looked up in alarm. 'Why? What's wrong with me?'

'We don't know that there is anything wrong with you at all. We want to get you checked out just to be on the safe side.'

'Lot of good having two of you here, then, isn't it?' Hew looked from one to the other. 'If neither of you can come up with any answers. Maybe I'd better see Dr Llewellyn.'

'He would say exactly the same as I'm saying,' said Aidan as he made a note to write a referral letter.

'I suppose that means going all the way into Bangor?' said Hew in obvious disgust.

'That's right, Hew. I'm sure your son will take you in,' Aidan replied briskly. 'Now, I also want you to have a blood test.'

Aidan carried on scribbling his notes so it was Lindsay who saw the frown cross the old man's features. 'There's nothing to worry about in having a blood test,' she said, reassuringly, she hoped.

'So who'll do it?' he demanded. 'Judith?'

Aidan carried on writing and Lindsay had to admit she didn't know.

'Fat lot of good that is,' said Hew in disgust. 'Call yourself a doctor and you don't even know a simple thing like that. You'll be telling me next you don't know who Judith is.' He gave a snort of disgust.

At that Aidan did look up and handed him a pink form for a blood test. 'Take that to the desk on your way out, Hew. You'll have to make an appointment because Judith only works here part time. And you'll receive your hospital appointment through the post in due course.'

Hew left the consulting room, still muttering to himself.

'So, are you going to tell me?' asked Lindsay as the door closed behind him.

'Tell you what?' Aidan turned to her and frowned.

'Who Judith is?'

'You mean you really don't know?'

'Of course I don't. How would I?' She shrugged.

He took a deep breath. 'I'm sorry,' he said. 'I thought perhaps Henry might have told you things like that. But he does have a lot on his mind at the moment so I guess perhaps there are many things you haven't been told. Judith is our practice nurse. She works part time here and part time in a practice in Betws-y-coed. You'll meet her later when she comes in. Right, we'd better get on or we'll never get through this surgery.' He pressed the buzzer.

'Let's hope this one takes a little more kindly to the fact that you have a trainee,' said Lindsay.

'You mustn't mind them too much. It's understandable they'll be a bit wary of a newcomer at first.'

'Especially someone all the way from London!' Lindsay pulled a face.

'You just wait until the word gets round—you'll be snowed under by those seeking second opinions.'

'I shouldn't count on it.' She stopped as someone knocked at the door and Aidan bade them enter.

This time the patient was a young woman with a baby. She looked startled at first to see Lindsay, but after the introductions and explanations she seemed pleased to have a woman there, especially as her problem concerned discomfort in her breasts after feeding her baby. By the end of the consultation she was addressing all her remarks to Lindsay while Aidan sat back in his chair and relaxed. The end result was that he allowed Lindsay to prescribe the cream that would alleviate the soreness of the nipples and tablets to help with the pain and discomfort.

'There you are, you see,' he said as the woman left the room. 'That's one satisfied customer.'

But it *was* only one and as the morning surgery wore on Lindsay found there were more patients who had the same suspicious attitude towards her as Hew Griffiths's than there were with that of the young mother's. It was with a decided sense of relief that at last she heard Bronwen buzz through and inform Aidan that he had no further patients for that particular surgery.

'Thank you, Bronwen.' He stretched and leaned back in his chair. 'Do I have many house calls?'

'Only four at the moment, Dr Lennox,' Bronwen replied in her precise tone.

He stood up and looked down at Lindsay.

'Do you want me to come with you?' she asked.

'I think you'd better. I was going to get Bronwen to show you a bit more of the workings of the place, but on second thoughts I think you'd be better off coming with me.'

Lindsay wasn't sure whether she was relieved or not

and which would have been the lesser evil—accompanying an obviously reluctant Aidan on his house calls or being forced to endure a couple of hours of the equally reluctant Bronwen's company.

In silence she slipped on her jacket, which she'd discarded during the surgery, then picked up her case and followed Aidan from the room. None of this was turning out as she'd expected. For the umpteenth time since arriving she felt like throwing her bags into the boot of her car and hightailing it back down the motorway to London.

'What do you have for me?' asked Aidan as they reached Reception and he moved behind the desk into the records section. Lindsay wasn't sure whether to follow him or not and in the end she let him go and discuss his house calls with Bronwen while she hovered in the waiting area, reading the posters on display to pass the time.

'I like your suit.'

Lindsay had become engrossed in one of the posters advertising a local helpline and she hadn't heard anyone come out of the records room. She looked round and found Gwynneth leaning over the counter and admiringly eyeing her up and down.

'Oh, do you? Thank you, Gwynneth. I was actually thinking just now that it's not really practical for country living.'

'I think it's lovely,' said Gwynneth. 'Did you buy it in London?'

'Er…yes. Yes, I did.' Lindsay nodded.

'Was it from Harrods?' asked Gwynneth in awe.

'No, it wasn't from Harrods.'

'Selfridges?' The dreamy look was back on Gwynneth's face.

'No. I bought it in a little boutique in Kensington.'

'Kensington!' Gwynneth's pale blue eyes rounded.

'Er…yes.' Lindsay nodded uncertainly and was actually relieved when Aidan suddenly strode round the desk with a bundle of records in his hand.

'Are you fit?' He spoke with hardly as much as a glance in her direction and, not waiting for a reply, strode to the front door.

'See you later, Gwynneth,' said Lindsay hastily, as with a little shrug she followed him.

'Yes,' replied Gwynneth wistfully. 'See you later…'

It had stopped raining and the cloud was lifting, leaving wraith-like strands around the tops of the mountains. There were several large puddles in the car park and Lindsay carefully circled them, protecting her neat black shoes from the water. Aidan led the way to his Land Rover climbed into the driver's seat then leaned across to open the passenger door for her.

'No dogs today?' she said nervously as she climbed in and shut the door behind her.

'They're at home,' he replied shortly. He started the engine and as they drew out of the car park it seemed he thought better of his somewhat curt answer and elaborated slightly. 'I'll call in and collect them—they usually come with me on my house calls then I let them have a run before afternoon surgery.'

Suddenly she was curious about his private life and where he lived. Really, she knew nothing—only that he was a doctor, drove a Land Rover and had two dogs. She didn't even know whether he was married or not. Henry had said he was a bit of a loner but that fact alone didn't mean he couldn't be married. She threw him a swift sidelong glance. His profile was set as he drew out of the forecourt onto the road, his brows drawn together in a frown of concentration. Her gaze moved to his hands on the wheel. Lindsay always looked at people's hands—they usually told so much about a person. Aidan's were square-shaped, capable-looking hands, and with their light covering of golden-tipped dark hairs, for some reason, appeared very, very masculine. Lindsay found herself looking quickly away.

The interior of the Land Rover smelt strongly of dog and Lindsay, unused to the smell, wrinkled her nose and surreptitiously opened her window a couple of inches.

'I've got four calls,' Aidan said, breaking the silence at last. 'First one is to an old couple who live just outside the village. The old boy has Parkinson's and his wife cares for him. She's a sweetie but her health isn't good and I'm not sure how much longer she'll be able to cope. I keep an eye on them and visit once a week.'

'What options will there be for them when she can no longer cope?' Lindsay half turned to him.

'It's difficult to say what will be best.' He gave a light shrug. 'We've talked over all the possibilities and I ended up promising them that when the time came I would do my utmost to get them somewhere they can stay together. He's deteriorating, though, and I fear the day's rapidly approaching when he'll need hospital or, at least, nursing-home care.'

'And his wife?' asked Lindsay.

'She isn't really bad enough to need that level of care but I wouldn't be happy for her to remain in the cottage on her own. Ideally she should go into a residential home, but it would break their hearts to be separated. It's a tough one.'

'How old are they?'

'Douglas is eighty-six and Milly is eighty-four. They celebrated their diamond wedding last week.'

While they'd been talking Aidan had driven through the village to the far side where the houses were further apart. Lindsay was just wondering which of the houses might be his when he pulled to the side of the road. 'Here we are,' he said. 'Want to come and see?'

Lindsay looked round. He'd actually stopped in a large gap between houses. Frowning, she climbed out of the Land Rover, slammed the door behind her and joined Aidan alongside the railings of a black iron fence.

'Watch the steps,' he said. 'They'll be wet and may be slippery.'

It was only then that she saw there was a gate set in the iron railings, and as Aidan opened the gate she leaned forward and saw the roof and chimneys of a building well below the level of the road. She followed him down the steps carefully because they were indeed slippery and her shoes had very little grip. Only when she reached the bottom did she look around her. The cottage, of grey stone and with a slate-tiled roof, was quite literally tucked into the hillside.

Aidan went on ahead of her and she heard the ecstatic welcome from his dogs as he opened the door of what appeared to be an outhouse. The dogs hurtled out and Lindsay steeled herself to greet them. Lindsay didn't actually dislike dogs but, having been nipped by a Jack Russell as a child, she was naturally wary. Aidan seemed to sense this as the dogs went overboard with their welcome, jumping around her as she stood uncertainly in the doorway.

'Skipper! Jess!' he rapped, and the dogs immediately

backed off before turning and rushing away into the garden.

'Sorry,' said Aidan, standing back so that Lindsay could enter the cottage. 'They get over-enthusiastic. I tend to forget not everyone is used to dogs.'

'I don't have a lot of dealings with dogs,' Lindsay admitted. 'It wouldn't do to keep one where I live.' She paused and looked around the kitchen. 'This is an interesting place you have. How long have you lived here?'

'Nearly three years,' he replied. 'And I'm still renovating it. I have a five-year plan. It was almost derelict when I first saw it so I've actually done more than you might think. Come and have a look at my most important find.' He led the way out of the kitchen with its beamed ceiling through a small dining room with a solid oak table and chairs and into a cosy sitting room. The walls were white and rough plastered and once again old beams had been restored, but behind the door and taking up the entire wall was a deep inglenook fireplace.

'That,' said Aidan proudly, 'had been bricked up. I discovered it quite by chance because one of the bricks was loose. Needless to say, when I saw what it was I ripped the entire wall out.'

'I'm impressed,' said Lindsay. 'I thought you only got those fireplaces in stately homes.'

'Apparently quite a few of these old cottages have them.'

'And is this your garden?' Lindsay had turned away from the fireplace and walked to the window.

'Wilderness would probably be a better description at the moment.' Aidan moved across the room and stood behind her. 'As you can imagine, the garden will probably be the last thing in the five-year plan.'

'But it's lovely,' said Lindsay slowly as she gazed out of the window. The garden, enclosed by a high stone wall, was indeed overgrown, but amongst the tangled mass of shrubs, plants and weeds were masses of wild flowers—large white daisies, buttercups, pink and white campion and tall foxgloves. Ivy tumbled over the wall and nasturtiums and scarlet geraniums grew from the cracks in the stonework. In one corner an old iron pump was half-submerged within a mass of creeping columbine and dog roses, while against the wall itself stood an ancient mangle, a further reminder of life in a bygone age. 'Is there another entrance?' Lindsay craned her neck.

Aidan nodded. 'Yes, there's a side road which leads to the lane at the front of the cottage where I keep the Land Rover, but if I'm in a hurry I tend to park on the road and come in the back way down the steps.'

'And the bedrooms?' mused Lindsay, stepping from the sittingroom and staring up the stairs.

'You want to see my bedroom?'

For probably the first time she caught a hint of amusement in his voice, and as she realised what she'd said she flushed. Passing swiftly over his question, she said, 'How many bedrooms do you have?'

'Two,' he replied. 'There were three but I'm afraid I settled for the modern option in this case and converted one into a bathroom. Want to take a look?'

'If we have the time,' she replied coolly. She did want to see because there was something about the whole place and what Aidan had done to it that really fascinated her, but on the other hand, she thought as

she followed him up the steep, narrow staircase, the
last thing she wanted him to think was that she was
keen to see the room just because it happened to be
his bedroom.

# CHAPTER FIVE

THERE was a large wooden bed in the main bedroom, its headboard and footrail of stylish stripped pine, its cover heavy white cotton. In here the walls were cream and the soft velvet curtains a bright delphinium-blue. Lindsay found herself staring at the king-sized bed and wondering anew if Aidan shared his life with anyone. There were no signs of feminine occupation—no clothes or cosmetics. It was just the bed, which really was very large, that gave her cause to wonder. As she stood in the bedroom doorway, looking round at the room, she fought to find something to say.

'Do you like it?' Aidan unexpectedly came to her rescue.

'I do,' she replied, nodding. 'Very much. I was just thinking how much Romilly would like it.'

'Romilly?' He frowned.

'Yes, she's my father's girlfriend. She also happens to be an interior designer—a very good one, actually.'

'Really?' He raised his eyebrows. 'And you say she's your father's girlfriend?'

'Yes, a long-term girlfriend. Oh, don't worry, this isn't a London den-of-vice case—my mother died many years ago when I was a child.'

'That was sad—for you especially, I mean.' He led the way out of the bedroom and opened the door of the second room which was still to be renovated and which appeared to be used as a storeroom. 'What happened?'

'She was involved in an accident,' Lindsay replied with a brief look at the room, understanding as she did so from the state of the walls just how much work Aidan must have put in on the rest of the cottage. 'A hit-and-run driver on a pedestrian crossing outside the house we lived in at that time. He was never caught,' she added briefly.

'I'm sorry.' He didn't sympathise or commiserate any further, like most people did on hearing of the tragic circumstances of her background, a fact for which she was grateful. It still hurt to talk about those terrible days when she'd been seven. 'Do you have brothers or sisters?' he asked instead.

'No.' She shook her head. 'There's just me—and my father. We moved to Chelsea soon after the accident, where my father still lives.'

'And you have your flat in Fulham.' His tone had changed slightly but she was uncertain of the implication in his tone. She threw him a sharp glance as, after she'd taken a quick look at the modernised bathroom, he stood back in order for her to descend the staircase ahead of him, but his expression was inscrutable.

'Yes,' she agreed lightly, 'I have my flat. And I'm glad of it. There's nothing like a bit of independence, as I'm sure you'll agree.' If she'd thought he might volunteer any information about the degree of his own independence she was mistaken for he declined even to reply.

Instead, once they reached the ground floor he said, 'I'd better round up those hounds, then we must be on our way.' Opening the door, he called to the dogs who appeared a moment later from the depths of the garden. By this time Lindsay had stepped from the cottage and was standing in the small courtyard outside the back door.

The two dogs bounded up to the cottage and too late Lindsay realised they were wet through from the grass and undergrowth. Before she had time to take evasive action they'd shaken themselves thoroughly, spraying her with a shower of water.

With a little cry she jumped backwards, at the same time trying to brush the water from her suit. If Aidan noticed, which she doubted, he said nothing. Fuming silently to herself, Lindsay preceded him up the steps, nearly losing her balance as the dogs streaked past and sat on the top step, panting noisily with their tongues hanging out as they waited for Aidan.

Without a word Lindsay climbed into the Land Rover. Aidan let the dogs into the back and almost immediately Lindsay felt a wet nose nuzzle the side of her neck. Turning her head sharply, she found Skipper, the Old English sheepdog, had his chin resting on the back of her seat.

'He really seems to have taken to you,' said Aidan with a glance over his shoulder as he secured his seat belt. 'He isn't usually so amiable with strangers.'

'Really?' Lindsay replied coolly.

It only took about five minutes to reach the home of Douglas and Milly Morgan. This, too, was a stone and slate cottage but one in a row of five others, all with immaculate front gardens and net curtains at the windows. Milly was watching out for them and had the front door open almost before they were out of the Land Rover.

'I thought you might be here today, Dr Lennox,' she said with a smile. She was a plump, apple-cheeked little woman whose appearance was as neat as that of her home. 'And who's this?' She turned an inquisitive but not unfriendly look at Lindsay.

'This is Dr Lindsay Henderson,' Aidan replied as they followed Milly into her tiny living room. 'She's come to join us at the practice for a while.'

'And where are you from, then?' asked Milly.

'I'm from London.' Lindsay braced herself as she waited for the usual adverse reaction which that particular confession seemed to bring forth.

'Ah,' said Milly. 'London.'

'Milly is from London, aren't you, Milly?' said Aidan.

'Many, many years ago,' Milly replied with a sigh as Lindsay turned to her in surprise. 'I was born and bred in London until a certain Welshman whisked me away to his native Wales.' She looked up at Lindsay. 'Tell me, how is the old city?'

'It was looking well when I left,' Lindsay replied, 'but, then, it's a lovely time of the year and the parks were all at their best.'

'So how is the Welshman today?' asked Aidan.

'He's about the same.' Milly shook her head. 'His nights are bad, though—he's very restless.'

'Let's have a look at him, Milly.'

Milly turned as if to lead the way into the next room, but before she could do so the door was pushed open and a Zimmer frame appeared, followed by an old man who shuffled forward, holding tightly to the frame.

'Hello, there, Douglas,' said Aidan. 'Nice to see you mobile today.'

While Milly bustled forward and helped her husband to a high-backed chair by the window Aidan put his case on the table and unlocked it. Lindsay, who was watching Douglas, saw the uncontrollable fit of shaking, so characteristic of sufferers of Parkinson's disease, that gripped him as he sank back into his chair. After a moment he turned his head in her direction, stretched out a still shaking hand and appeared to be trying desperately to say something.

'You want to know who this young lady is who's come to see you, don't you, Douglas?' said Aidan with an unexpected chuckle. 'She's a doctor and her name is Lindsay Henderson.' As he spoke, he handed Lindsay Douglas Morgan's records containing his care plan and medication chart.

'Dr Henderson comes from London,' announced Milly, before bustling away to the kitchen to brew some tea.

Lindsay took Douglas's hand in hers. 'I'm pleased to meet you, Mr Morgan,' she said. She didn't let go of his hand immediately, and as she held it, while Aidan read through Douglas's latest hospital reports, she looked around the small but spotlessly clean living room. There were photographs everywhere—pictures of children and presumably grandchildren and great-grandchildren. There were framed wedding photographs, christening pictures, one of a young man in a mortarboard and gown and above the sideboard a faded, black-and-white photograph of a bride in a two-piece costume and feathered hat, with her handsome groom in army uniform. A whole lifetime of memories were there in that room.

Lindsay looked at Douglas and saw the tears had come to his eyes as he'd watched her follow the path of his and Milly's lives. Briefly, before she let go of his hand she gently squeezed it.

'I'm going to give him a light sedative at night,' murmured Aidan, looking up from the notes he was reading. 'Hopefully, that way they'll both get some rest. I don't want Milly getting too tired. There are some days when Douglas is bedridden and Milly has to do literally everything for him. Her angina has been worse this last winter and it's all taking its toll.' He handed Lindsay the records and while she was studying them Milly came back into the room. Aidan rose swiftly to his feet to relieve her of the tray she carried.

'Milly, you've been baking again,' he said as he set the tray down on the table. Glancing at Lindsay, he added, 'Milly makes the best Welsh oatcakes you've ever tasted.'

'I'm not sure I've ever tasted Welsh oatcakes,' said Lindsay, shaking her head.

'Then your education is incomplete,' said Aidan solemnly.

Milly had started to pour the tea but at this interchange she set the teapot down and picked up a plate of the delicious-looking oatcakes. 'You will try one?' she said.

'How could I possibly refuse?' said Lindsay with a laugh. Only moments later, however, as she bit into one of the cookies, she knew that for once she and Aidan had found something they were in complete agreement about.

They stayed with the Morgans for a further ten minutes then when the pot was drained and the plate empty they took their leave, Aidan telling Milly that he would call in again in a week's time unless she needed anything before that. 'I'll drop the prescription into the chemist,' he said as Milly showed them to the door, 'then Elspeth can bring it home with her when she finishes work.'

'Who's Elspeth?' asked Lindsay as they took their

seats in the Land Rover to the accompaniment of an enthusiastic greeting from Skipper and Jess.

'She's a neighbour,' Aidan explained. 'She works in the butcher's shop, which is next to the chemist in the village. Roma, who's the pharmacist's assistant, will take the prescription to Elspeth before she goes home.' He paused and glared indignantly at Lindsay. 'Why are you laughing?' he demanded.

'I'm not,' she said. 'Not really. It's just that it's all so informal here, with everyone knowing everyone else. What you've just described would never happen in a million years in London. So much is so different here from what I'd expected...'

He was silent for a moment then, after he'd executed a perfect U-turn in the road, he said, 'So, are you going to tell me why it bothered you when you found out I was to be your trainer?'

For one moment the unexpectedness of the question took her breath away. 'I...well,' she floundered, 'I don't know that it exactly...'

'Yes, it did,' he said bluntly. 'You said it did. Last night at Henry's when I asked you if it was important to you that we should have got off to a good start, you said that it might have helped if we had, especially when you found out that I was to be your trainer. And then I asked you if it had bothered you, finding that out, and you said, and correct me if I'm wrong but I think your exact words were, "Actually, yes, it did if you must know." But that was as far as you got because Henry came back into the room at that moment.'

'All right.' Lindsay took a deep breath and raised her hand in a quick submissive gesture. 'That's right. I did say that.'

'And did you mean it?'

'As it happens, yes, I did.'

'So are you going to enlighten me as to why it should bother you so much?' he demanded. 'After all, let's face it, you'd only just met me so on that fact alone it seemed a pretty sweeping statement to make.'

'It probably had more to do with the fact that Henry was no longer to be my trainer than the fact that you were,' she admitted tightly at last.

'So are you saying it had nothing to do with me at all?'

'Actually, no, I'm not saying that. If you must know, I was still annoyed with you for not introducing yourself in the shop. Oh, I know you said you thought I was a tourist and I suppose I might give you the benefit of the doubt over that, but you must have realised who I was later, at the scene of the accident, and you should have said then who you were. From your behaviour I can only assume that you weren't too happy to have me in Tregadfan which automatically leads me to conclude you weren't too keen to have been landed with the job of my trainer. Am I right or not?' she demanded when he remained silent.

'Actually, yes,' he said at last. 'Absolutely right.'

'Well, that's charming.' She did nothing to disguise the sarcasm in her voice. 'Now we know exactly where we stand. You didn't want me here. You don't want to be my trainer, and I'm fed up because I had set my heart on Henry being my trainer.'

They were silent for a moment then Aidan spoke again. 'The only reason I didn't want you here was because I didn't happen to think the practice would benefit from a trainee. I didn't think it was the right time and, as it turned out, I was absolutely right. I went along with Henry in the end because it was what he wanted and I didn't think it would affect me too much. When Megan became so ill I thought Henry would drop the whole idea but, no, he didn't want to disappoint you so he asked—practically begged—me to take you on. I agreed in the end simply because I think Henry has enough stress at the moment with Megan, without adding to it.'

'Well, I wish someone had contacted me and asked me what I wanted,' retorted Lindsay.

'What would you have done if we had?' Aidan threw her a curious glance.

'I wouldn't have come. It's as simple as that. The only reason I've come all this way is because I wanted Henry to be my trainer. He's my godfather and ever since I was a child I've looked up to him and admired him. Had I known what was to happen I would have found another practice to take me on—probably one nearer home.'

'I thought you said you wanted to get out amongst ordinary people…'

'I could do that in London—it isn't all Harley Street, you know. There are plenty of areas where I would have gained experience of real life.'

They were silent again while Aidan drove back through the village then took a sharp left-hand corner and drove out onto the main road.

'So,' said Lindsay after a while, 'was your only reason for not wanting me here to do with the good of the practice, or was there anything against me personally?' When he didn't answer she said, 'Come on, fair's fair. You asked me the same question and I answered you.'

He took a deep breath. 'All right,' he said. 'If you must know, I didn't think you'd fit in here. I thought you looked totally unsuitable.'

'Why?' she demanded.

'Everything,' he said. 'Everything about you—your clothes, your style, your hair, even your car—it all smacked of wealth and privilege.'

'So you were ready to condemn me on appearances alone?'

He shrugged. 'Condemn's a strong word. Let's just say I thought you would find it very difficult to fit in with the folk in Tregadfan. And, I'll be honest, I thought that the moment I set eyes on you...'

'In the village shop?'

'Yes.'

'There you are, I said you knew who I was.' Her voice rose and there came a low growl from the back of the Land Rover.

'Quiet, Jess.' Aidan only spoke softly but there was no further sound from the Border collie. 'Let's just say I guessed. And my fears were proven.'

'Well, you weren't the only one with fears or misgivings,' she snapped. 'I can tell you I very nearly hightailed it straight back to London.'

'But you didn't.'

'No,' she admitted. 'I didn't.'

'May I ask why?'

'Because I also didn't want to upset Henry. He'd obviously gone to a lot of trouble and he's so worried about Megan...'

'So our feelings on that score are obviously the same.' He drove on in silence.

'Look,' said Lindsay after a moment, 'it seems as if we're stuck with this situation whether we like it or not. I guess we'll just have to put up with a bad job and get on with it.'

'Yes.' He nodded. 'I guess. But...'

'But what?' She threw him a sharp glance but his face was expressionless.

'May I make one suggestion?'

'What's that?'

'That you get yourself some decent shoes.'

'What's wrong with my shoes?' she demanded.

'Nothing,' he said. 'There's nothing wrong with your shoes at all and I'm sure they are absolutely perfect in London, but they're hardly practical for house calls in and around Tregadfan.'

She was still smarting from his criticism when they reached the address of the next patient. This time it was the home of Janet Pearce, a middle-aged woman whose elderly mother was bedridden after suffering a stroke. The patient was experiencing problems with digestion and diarrhoea and was suffering from the long-term effects of depression. After he'd examined her, Aidan turned to Janet.

'I'll give you a reflux suppressant which will help control her heartburn,' he said, 'and 2-mg capsules of loperamide hydochloride for the diarrhoea. Now, you say you feel her depression is worse?'

'Yes.' Janet nodded. 'She's very lethargic and tearful and barely sleeps at night.'

'In that case we'll take her off lofepramine and try sertraline,' he replied. Lindsay watched as Aidan wrote out the prescription for the new medication and handed it to Janet. She didn't comment until they'd left the house and were in the Land Rover once more.

'You got rather technical in there with that poor woman,' she observed.

'Janet, you mean?' He raised his eyebrows.

Lindsay nodded. 'Yes, all those generic drug names—she must have been quite bewildered.'

'So you're assuming that because Janet is at home, caring for her sick mother in this remote Welsh village of ours, she's never had any formal education, no life of her own?'

'I didn't say that!' Lindsay felt her face redden at the implication.

'But it's what you thought, isn't it?' he demanded as Jess began to fidget in the back.

'No. It isn't, as it happens. I merely thought she may have found it confusing. I very rarely use generic names when I'm talking to patients—*any* patients. They recognise proprietary brand names far more readily.'

'And what about when you're talking to fellow members of the medical profession?' he asked coolly.

'Well, that's different. Of course it is, but—'

'So what would you say if I were to tell you that Janet was a staff nurse in the general hospital in Bangor for many years before she left to care for her mother?'

Lindsay drew in her breath sharply. 'I would say you should have told me either before we reached the house or when you introduced her to me. I would have said it would have been common courtesy to do so.'

Aidan didn't answer, merely swung the Land Rover onto the forecourt of the surgery and switched off the engine.

'I thought you had four house calls,' she said sharply.

'I do.' His reply was terse. 'But one is only to call in to see Tom again at the Red Dragon and the other is to a remote farm, which I shall do this evening before I go home. Besides, I thought you might have had enough.'

'I may not be used to your weather or your country

ways,' she snapped, 'but I'm more than capable of coping with a few house calls. I can assure you this is a doddle compared with what I was used to on a busy day in Accident and Emergency.'

He shrugged. 'I'm not disputing that. I have, after all, done my own stint as a houseman. I simply thought you might be glad of some time to get yourself settled into the flat.'

'I haven't even seen the flat yet,' she protested. 'It may not be suitable.'

'I can assure you it's entirely suitable.'

His arrogance almost took her breath away. 'How do you know what may or may not be suitable for me?' she demanded as she felt her temper rising.

'You're forgetting I lived in the flat when my place was uninhabitable. It suited me admirably so I fail to see why it shouldn't suit you.' Opening the door, he jumped to the ground, slammed the door and strode off across the road to the Red Dragon, leaving her sitting in the Land Rover with the dogs, quietly seething. How she was to be expected to work with this man for the next year she had no idea.

At last, with a sigh, she turned to the dogs. 'I suppose you're used to him,' she said. She received solemn, doleful looks in return before she, too, climbed from the Land Rover. After checking that Aidan had left his window open for air for the dogs, she made her way into the surgery.

Bronwen was seated at her desk behind the reception counter and was typing, while Gwynneth appeared to be filing notes. They both looked up as she came in.

'Oh, there you are,' said Gwynneth. 'We were just talking about you. Here she is, Bronwen. She's back.'

'Yes, Gwynneth, thank you,' Bronwen replied frostily. 'I can see that. Where's Dr Lennox?' She eyed Lindsay up and down as if she suspected her of spiriting Aidan away somewhere.

'He's gone across to the Red Dragon to see someone called Tom.'

'Tom's the landlord,' explained Gwynneth. 'He was very poorly in the night. He's got emphysema—'

'Yes, all right, thank you, Gwynneth,' said Bronwen sharply. 'We don't discuss patients' details in Reception where we can be overheard, do we?'

'No...' Gwynneth looked around. 'But there's only Dr Henderson here.'

'Nevertheless, it does well to refrain at all times, otherwise we get into bad habits. Now, Dr Henderson,' Bronwen went on briskly, 'your flat is ready. Would you care to see it now?'

'Yes, I may as well,' Lindsay replied. 'I don't seem to be required for anything else at the moment.'

'Very well.' Bronwen stood up and walked briskly round the counter to join her, but as they began to walk towards the staircase at the end of the hall a sudden cry from Gwynneth stopped them.

'Dr Henderson! Oh, Dr Henderson!' She ran round the counter, flapping her hands. 'Oh, your beautiful suit!'

'My suit?' Lindsay stopped. 'What's wrong with my suit?'

'It's covered in dogs' hair.' Gwynneth reached them and began trying to brush down Lindsay's suit with her hands.

'Dogs' hair,' said Lindsay flatly. 'Now, why doesn't that surprise me?'

# CHAPTER SIX

LINDSAY was half expecting the flat to be awful—in fact, she was secretly hoping it would be just so that she could have the pleasure of telling Aidan so—but as Bronwen showed her around Lindsay was reluctantly forced to admit that it was ideal for her needs. Both the sitting room and the one bedroom had mountain views, with the peak of Snowdon itself as the focal point. There was a well-equipped kitchen with a small dining area and an adequate bath and shower room. The fittings and furnishings were basic and in mainly neutral tones.

'I'm sure you'll want to add some personal touches of your own,' said Bronwen.

'I didn't bring very much with me,' Lindsay replied, 'because, of course, I thought I would be staying with Dr and Mrs Llewellyn. But, yes, you're right, I like a few bright colours about the place so I'll buy some bits and pieces. Speaking of which, there are a few other things I need—maybe you can point me in the direction of some shops.'

'What sort of things?' Bronwen frowned.

'Clothes, really.'

Bronwen's gaze travelled briefly over her suit and stylish black shoes. 'I doubt we have anything round here that would appeal to you,' she replied stiffly.

'Oh, I don't mean anything like this,' Lindsay replied. 'I mean something more suited to life in

Tregadfan. It's already been pointed out to me that my attire is totally unsuitable, or at least my shoes are.'

'In that case, you could try taking a trip into Betws-y-coed. There are several clothes shops there that sell good, serviceable clothes and shoes.'

'Thank you, Bronwen. I'll do that.' She paused. 'Now, can I move in here right away?'

'I don't see why not.' Bronwen shrugged. 'The bed is made up and the place has been kept aired.'

'In that case, I think this afternoon if Dr Lennox doesn't need me. I'll pop back to the house and fetch the rest of my things then do a bit of shopping.'

'Don't worry about Dr Lennox,' said Bronwen. 'I'll tell him where you've gone.' She spoke in a way that implied she could more than handle any problem with Aidan.

Not for the first time it crossed Lindsay's mind that the rather formidable Bronwen might have a soft spot for Aidan Lennox. It would certainly explain why she'd appeared hostile to Lindsay's appearance on the scene. No doubt she would appear hostile to any woman who was about to claim any part of Aidan's attention.

While she was driving back to the Llewellyns' house Lindsay's thoughts returned briefly to Bronwen. She wondered if she was right about the receptionist's feelings toward Aidan and if that were the case whether they were in any way reciprocated. Somehow she found that hard to imagine. There hadn't been the slightest indication on Aidan's part that there was any relationship between himself and Bronwen other than that of employer and employee, but on the other hand maybe he insisted on that professional-type approach at the surgery.

Maybe, away from work, it was a different matter.

Maybe then Bronwen would let her hair down and
Aidan would relax and laugh… And perhaps that was
the reason for that huge bed in his cottage…

As an image of Aidan and Bronwen together in an
intimate situation flitted through her mind Lindsay
found that, far from being amused at the idea, she
found it oddly disturbing and she dismissed it before it
had time to take hold.

Henry had gone home to have lunch with Megan.
Lindsay met him in the hall on his way back to the
surgery.

'Lindsay, my dear.' He looked harassed. 'Is everything all right?'

'Yes, of course. I've just come back to collect my
things.'

'You're going to move into the flat?'

'Yes…'

'Have you seen it?' Henry looked anxious. 'Do you
think you'll be comfortable there?'

'Yes, I have seen it. It's fine, Henry. Please, stop
worrying. I'm sure I'll be perfectly all right there. I'm
going into Betws-y-coed to buy a few bits and pieces.'
She paused. 'How's Megan?'

'About the same. You'll go in and see her before
you go?'

'Of course.'

'Well, I'd best get back. I have an antenatal clinic
this afternoon.' Henry turned to open the front door
then he stopped, one hand on the latch. 'Oh, Lindsay
how did your first morning go?'

'OK, I think.' She shrugged. 'Although maybe you'd
better check with Aidan about that.'

'Why?' Henry frowned.

'Well, his opinion may well be vastly different from mine,' Lindsay replied with a tight little smile.

'Lindsay, you mustn't let Aidan bother you,' said Henry slowly. 'He can appear rather aloof at times and, like I told you, he's a bit of a loner, but—'

'He really is very nice when you get to know him...' With a laugh Lindsay finished the sentence for him. 'I know, Henry,' she added gently when she saw his expression change to one of anxiety again. 'Don't worry about Aidan and me. I'm sure we'll get along.

'Eventually,' she added under her breath as she watched Henry climb into his car and disappear down the drive.

She found Megan quite tearful at the fact that she wasn't to be staying with them.

'It doesn't matter, Megan, really it doesn't,' Lindsay hastened to reassure the older woman. 'I'll be quite all right in the flat.'

'But it isn't at all what we'd planned. We wanted you to be one of the family during your stay in Tregadfan. It would have been like having one of the children home again... And now...now, because of me...it's all ruined. I know Henry is disappointed. It isn't what he wanted at all.'

'You mustn't worry, Megan. I'm sure all Henry is concerned about is your health and having you well again.'

'But he saw this as a way of repaying your father. He was very good to Henry in the past—'

'Megan, whatever it was, my father won't want to be repaid. Henry is his friend. Now, come on.' Sitting on the side of the bed, Lindsay put her arm around Megan's shoulders in a further attempt to comfort her. 'You mustn't upset yourself like this. I'm perfectly all right. The flat is fine, I'll come and see you as often as I can and I'll still be doing my training, even though it's with Aidan...'

'Do you get on all right with Aidan?' Megan lowered her handkerchief and looked anxiously at Lindsay.

'Get on with Aidan? Well, it's early days yet but, yes, I'm sure it'll be all right. Besides, why shouldn't I?'

'Well, he can be a bit difficult at times, I know...'

'I won't let that bother me. It'll be fine, Megan. Really, it will. You're not to worry about it.' She paused, hesitating, then as casually as she could she said, 'Talking of Aidan, he's not married or anything, is he?'

'No.' Megan shook her head. 'He isn't married, neither, as far as I know, is there anyone in his life at the moment. There was someone...once, but that was a long time ago...'

'You're getting tired, Megan,' said Lindsay in concern. 'I'd better go and let you sleep.'

'Yes, in a moment. I'm fed up with sleeping. I want to talk to you for a bit. Tell me, Lindsay, dear, there isn't anyone in your life at the moment, is there?'

Lindsay shook her head. 'No, not now,' she said. 'But how did you know?'

'I think your father mentioned it when he spoke to Henry. He said the reason you'd postponed your training was because of your relationship with... with...what was his name...?'

'Andrew,' Lindsay replied quietly.

'Yes, Andrew. That was it. And that as the relationship had now ended he wondered if Henry would still be interested in taking you on as a trainee.' Megan paused. 'So what happened between you and Andrew?'

'It didn't work out,' Lindsay replied with a little

shrug. She tried to appear nonchalant but inside it felt as if her heart had twisted, the way it always did at any mention of Andrew. 'It was just one of those things,' she said. 'It wasn't meant to be. It was as simple as that.'

'Never mind,' said Megan gently, her lovely eyes full of concern. 'There will be someone else for you, Lindsay, and very soon, I should think—just you wait and see. Why, who knows, maybe even you and Aidan—?'

'No, Megan, no.' She spoke more sharply than she'd meant to and Megan's eyes widened. 'No,' she said again, but less emphatically this time. 'We're complete opposites and, besides, the last thing I'm looking for at the moment is another relationship.'

She left Megan to rest after that and drove to Betws-y-coed. The rain and cloud of earlier had cleared, giving way to the sort of May day that gave one that good-to-be-alive feeling. The sun was warm, the trees resplendent in their new fresh growth and in the fields that season's lambs leapt and played. The hillsides were a mass of purple rhododendrons and the moorland verges thick with heather and yellow broom.

As she drove, Lindsay played the latest CD by The Corrs and, humming along to the music, she felt her spirits lift at last. Maybe things wouldn't be as bad as she had feared. It seemed she had no choice other than to get used to Aidan Lennox and his ways, but at least the flat was nice and she would have her independence.

The shops in Betws-y-coed were quite obviously geared to the tourist trade, but in a way that suited Lindsay very well because, after all, wasn't that what she was—simply a visitor to the area? A visitor who needed to gear herself to the demands of the location.

She found a rather nice shop that sold practical clothing, where she bought herself a couple of pairs of hard-wearing trousers, two cotton sweaters and a waterproof waxed jacket. She'd brought skirts with her which she could team up with the sweaters for work, but for good measure she also bought a couple of shirts. In the adjoining shop she found a pair of sensible walking shoes, smiling to herself as she tried them on, tying the laces and wondering what her friends in London would have thought if they could have seen her.

Well pleased with her purchases, she was on her way back to the car park when she passed a shop selling home furnishings. On a sudden impulse she went inside and half an hour later came out with a lampshade, two throw-overs, a framed print, a selection of brightly coloured vases and an assortment of dried twigs, flowers and driftwood. Somehow, laden with huge carrier bags, she staggered back to the car.

Gwynneth seemed even more nervous than usual when Lindsay arrived back at the surgery. 'Oh,' she said as Lindsay carried her purchases into Reception, 'there you are. We wondered—'

'That's enough, Gwynneth.' Swiftly Bronwen intervened. 'I trust you found what you required in Betws-y-coed?'

'Yes, thanks.' Lindsay nodded. 'I think you'll find I'm better equipped now for whatever Tregadfan flings at me, whether it's rain, mud, hail, sleet or snow.'

'We don't very often have snow at this time of the year,' said Gwynneth seriously.

'Get on with your work,' Gwynneth,' snapped Bronwen.

Upstairs in the flat Lindsay unpacked her shopping, sorted out her clothes and hung them up in the large oak wardrobe in the bedroom or laid them in the drawers of the matching chest. On further exploration she found that the flat was very well equipped with linen and towels and she spent the next hour happily rearranging things to her taste, positioning the brightly coloured throw-overs on the sofa and armchair, replacing the rather gloomy picture in her bedroom with the print she'd bought and filling the vases and containers with the dried arrangements of twigs and flowers.

At last everything was as she wanted it and she gazed around the flat in satisfaction. It was only then that she realised she had no food and that really she should be thinking of going to the village shop. She'd not yet explored the possibility of other alternatives, such as eating out, although somehow she doubted whether Tregadfan had much to offer in the way of night life. There had been several veiled allusions to the fact that things would change drastically with the coming of the May bank holiday and a sudden influx of tourists, but until then she couldn't see there was much in the way of local excitement.

If she'd been at home she would have been looking forward to an evening out, clubbing with friends from the hospital or visiting a wine bar with Annabelle. As she thought of her friend she decided to call her.

Annabelle answered on the tenth ring. 'You sound breathless,' said Lindsay with a chuckle. 'What have I interrupted?'

'Lindsay!' Annabelle's shriek could probably have been heard in Betws-y-coed. 'What a lovely surprise! Where are you?'

In the depths of Welsh Wales, of course—where do you think?'

'Oh, God, is it utterly ghastly?' demanded Annabelle.

'If you'd asked me that question last night I would probably have said yes and that I was seriously thinking of coming home. However, it has got better. Only a fraction, but today it has got better. How long it lasts remains to be seen.'

'So tell me. I want to know. Why was it ghastly?'

'Well, the village folk treat me like I've just landed from another planet, Henry Llewellyn's wife is ill and he's no longer able to be my trainer and he's arranged for his partner—a guy called Aidan Lennox—to take me on.'

'And are you happy with that?' asked Annabelle.

'I'll have to see how it goes—let's just say Aidan Lennox isn't the sort of person one warms to immediately. I've also decided not to impose on the Llewellyns by staying with them so I've moved into a flat over the surgery.'

'Oh, Lindsay, it sounds appalling. For God's sake, why don't you just chuck it in and come home?'

'I can't, Annabelle. Henry and Megan are upset enough as it is. If I go home it'll make them feel worse than ever. I must stick it out—at least, for a while. Obviously if it gets too bad I'll have to think again.'

'So what's the village like? Is it absolutely dire?'

'No, actually, that's the one saving grace. The village is beautiful, Belle. It's surrounded by mountains— you should see the views I've got from this flat.'

'But what about the people?' Annabelle still sounded doubtful.

'I haven't met too many yet. Some of the patients seem wary of anyone from London.' She sighed. 'And then there's the staff. A woman called Bronwen who rules the surgery with a rod of iron and a poor little mouse of a receptionist who's terrified of her…'

'And what about this guy who's your new trainer—what's he like?'

'Aidan? Well, he's not quite what we're used to, Belle.'

'A nerd, you mean?

'No, not a nerd,' she said slowly. 'Different maybe, but not a nerd. He's too clued up for that.'

'So in what way different?' Annabelle persisted.

'It's hard to explain really. When I first saw him with his Land Rover and his dogs, his waxed jacket and green wellies I thought he was a farmer.'

'Sounds a tad interesting. Is he hunky?'

'Lord, no. Nothing like that. Rugged maybe, but not hunky. More irritating really. I dare say he'll have driven me mad by the end of a week.'

'Not your type, then?'

'No. Definitely not my type.'

'Oh, well, never mind.' Annabelle sighed. 'It was just a thought. Speaking of which, and I don't know whether you'll want to know this or not…'

'Try me.'

'Well, I saw Andrew today. I was just coming out of Harvey Nic's and there he was.'

Lindsay clutched the phone a little tighter. 'Go on,' she said.

'We stopped, passed the time of day and he…he asked after you. I told him you'd gone away and he seemed surprised. Hadn't you told him, Lindsay—about Wales, I mean?'

'He knew it was on the cards, but I didn't make up my mind until after we'd split.'

'Would you have gone if you and Andrew had still been together?'

'Probably not.'

'That's what I thought. Anyway, he said to say hello.'

And that, Lindsay thought as a little later she replaced the receiver, was all it had come down to between her and Andrew—him saying hello through a friend. There had been a time, and not so long ago either, when she'd thought he'd been the love of her life but that had been then, before she'd found out that fidelity in a relationship hadn't seemed to feature on his agenda. She'd forgiven him the first time when she'd quite by chance seen him dining out with an attractive woman. As Annabelle had pointed out when she'd confided in her, it hadn't been as if she and Andrew had been living together then, or engaged, or anything like that. But the second time had been different. By then they'd been living together, a commitment had been made, and she'd found out in the most hurtful way that he'd been seeing someone else.

She'd hoped she'd been starting to get over it but hearing Annabelle refer to having seen him again, casual though it might have been, had really upset her.

With her thoughts still churning, Lindsay made her way downstairs with the intention of braving the village shop and its strange inhabitants to buy some food. Bronwen and Gwynneth were clearing up and the last patient was just leaving the surgery.

Lindsay would have let herself out of the front door without disturbing the two receptionists, but as she reached the door Bronwen suddenly spoke. 'Dr Henderson,' she said briskly, 'Dr Lennox wants to see you.'

Lindsay looked at her watch. 'I was about to go to the village shop to buy some food. It's nearly five o'clock.'

'Dr Lennox said to be sure to tell you at the end of surgery. He's just seen his last patient. You'd better go in to him now.'

'Right.' Lindsay took a deep breath and glanced across the hall to Aidan's room. The door was tightly shut.

'It's all right, Dr Henderson.' Gwynneth suddenly spoke as Lindsay still hesitated. 'The shop doesn't close until six.'

'Thanks, Gwynneth.' Lindsay shot her a grateful glance then, squaring her shoulders, she walked briskly to Aidan's room and rapped smartly on the door.

He barely had a chance to bid her to enter before she pushed open the door. He was seated behind his desk, writing, but he looked up sharply at the interruption, his pen poised. His gaze met hers and unexpectedly, although she wasn't sure why, she felt her heart miss a beat.

She drew a deep breath. 'You wanted to see me?' she said abruptly, only too mindful of the interchange of words they'd had at the end of the morning.

'Yes,' he replied tautly. 'I did. I wanted an explanation as to why you weren't in surgery this afternoon.'

She stared at him. 'I went shopping,' she replied.

'You went shopping.' It was a statement rather than a question. 'May I ask if you intend doing that sort of thing on a regular basis? Because if you do, I might as well say here and now that I don't intend continuing as your trainer.'

Lindsay felt the blood rush to her cheeks, then as she turned to shut the door behind her, very briefly she caught sight of a half-smile on Bronwen's face. Struggling to control her temper, she strode across Aidan's consulting room and placed her hands, palms downwards, on his desk. 'Right,' she said. 'Now that your smug receptionist can no longer hear us, maybe you'll tell me what the hell this is all about.'

'You know what it's about,' he replied coldly. 'I expected you here in surgery this afternoon and you chose to go shopping without so much as a by your leave.'

'But you more or less said you didn't need me any more, that you thought I might have things to do…'

'That was this morning! I didn't think you would see fit to take the rest of the day off.'

'Bronwen knew where I was,' she retorted. 'In fact, it was she who suggested I go into Betws-y-coed for the shopping I needed.'

'Shall we leave Bronwen out of this—'

'But she was to tell you where I'd gone and why.'

'Maybe so, but the point I'm making is that you should have told me.'

'Told you? Don't you mean, asked you?' Her tone was now as cold as his. 'I wasn't aware that I was to be accountable to you for every minute of every day.'

'I'm not saying you are, but I do need to know when you intend doing surgeries or house calls. Surely you must see that.'

Struggling for control, Lindsay drew a deep breath. 'OK,' she said at last, 'I accept that because you are my trainer maybe I should have mentioned it to you first.'

'If you had, there would have been no problem. I'm not so insensitive that I can't understand there would be things you needed to do on your first day here.' He paused and for a long moment he stared up at her.

His eyes seemed more bluer than ever. 'We really don't seem to have got off to a good start, do we?' he said tightly at last.

'No.' She shook her head, only too aware that her face was still flushed. 'We don't. We seem to have been at odds with each other since the moment we met, and it will go on like that if you carry on treating me like a naughty schoolgirl. I may only be the trainee in this practice but I also happen to be a fully qualified doctor and I expect to be treated as such.'

Aidan continued to stare at her with that disconcerting blue gaze then quietly he said, 'May I make a suggestion?' When she gave a little shrug he went on, 'Shall we start again?'

'What do you mean?' Her eyes narrowed.

'What I say. Shall we go back to the beginning? Pretend we've just met and this time try and get off on the right foot. What do you say?'

She hesitated. 'All right.' She nodded.

He stood up and held out his hand. 'Dr Aidan Lennox,' he said briefly. 'I'm to be your trainer for the next year.'

'Dr Lindsay Henderson.' She took his hand, aware as she did so of its unexpected warmth, so at odds with the ice blue of his eyes.

## CHAPTER SEVEN

GRADUALLY, over the next couple of weeks, things got better. Lindsay settled into her flat and it soon began to feel like home. In the practice staff and patients alike began to accept her and she in turn got used to them. Aidan continued to irritate her at times but she was sure that she also irritated him. At other times she found him profoundly disconcerting, and yet as time went by they each made a concerted effort to accommodate the other.

She still found Bronwen infuriating and she knew Bronwen only tolerated her presence in the surgery, but surprisingly Gwynneth proved to be an unexpected ally. It was obvious that Gwynneth had always gone in fear and trepidation of Bronwen, treating the older woman with a deference far beyond her due, and when she saw that Lindsay had no intention of doing likewise, her awe and admiration for the new trainee knew no bounds.

'You mustn't let her get to you,' Lindsay told the girl when she found her in tears behind the filing cabinets one morning after a particularly hurtful run-in with Bronwen.

'I...I c-can't help it...' Gwynneth hiccuped. 'She makes me feel so stupid all the time.'

'You're not stupid, Gwynneth,' said Lindsay gently. 'And Bronwen has no right to make you feel as if you are. If you like, I'll have a word with Dr Llewellyn.'

'Oh, no,' gasped Gwynneth, 'you mustn't do that.

After all, Bronwen is senior receptionist here. She would only make things even more difficult for me if she thought I'd been telling tales.'

'But you are also an employee here and I know for a fact that neither Dr Llewellyn nor Dr Lennox, for that matter, would want you to be miserable.'

'Oh, you mustn't tell Dr Lennox either. You won't, will you?' Gywnneth demanded, her eyes wide with panic.

'Of course not. Not if you don't want me to,' Lindsay replied, but at the same time she resolved that if she could do anything to make the girl's working conditions a little happier she would do so.

She'd continued sitting in on Aidan's surgeries as she'd got to know the ropes until during her second week they reversed roles and he sat in while she took a few of his surgeries. This brought mixed reactions from the patients. There were those who flatly refused to discuss their problems with her, and although she remained in the room all their comments were addressed to Aidan as if she were invisible and he was the one conducting the surgery. Luckily these cases were few and far between and most people seemed willing to give her a chance once the situation had been satisfactorily explained to them.

And then, of course, there were those, just as Aidan had predicted, who were only too delighted to have the luxury of a second opinion, and while these cases presented Lindsay with something she could get her teeth into, they also proved controversial if her diagnosis differed from Aidan's or Henry's.

Aidan continued to sit in on her surgeries and Lindsay found herself longing for the day when she could be on her own. It wasn't that he interfered. In fact, most of the time he was so quiet that one could almost have forgotten that he was there—anyone but herself, that was—for no matter how quiet or unobtrusive he was Lindsay found it impossible to ignore his presence.

Most of the time she found she was waiting for him to intervene, and even though he didn't his presence alone made her wonder about every statement or piece of advice she gave and certainly about every diagnosis she made. It was as if she consciously expected him to disagree with her, and when he didn't her surprise almost threw her.

'How's it going?' asked Judith after one particularly tense surgery when Lindsay crashed out in the staff-room with a strong coffee.

'Let's just say it's times like this I wish I smoked,' Lindsay replied tautly.

'Bad as that?' Judith pulled a sympathetic face.

'Not bad exactly.' Lindsay stared into her mug. 'Let's just say I have to be constantly on my toes.'

'I know the feeling.' Judith nodded. 'When I first came here I imagined Aidan was laid-back and easy-going, probably because of his dress and his lifestyle—you know what I mean, taking those dogs around everywhere with him—but I soon learned that when it comes down to his work he's an absolute perfectionist.'

'You can say that again.' Lindsay sighed and brushed back a strand of hair which had escaped from the slide she wore at the nape of her neck. 'I find myself waiting for him to comment after every word I utter. Usually he doesn't—but that still doesn't stop me being on edge.'

'I bet you wish you were with Henry, don't you?'

'You could say that. I'm sure that, working with

Henry, I would have known where I was. As it is, with Aidan I feel I'm walking on eggshells all the time.' Draining her mug, she stood up only to find that, unbeknown to either herself or Judith, Aidan had come quietly into the staffroom and had probably heard every word she'd said.

She worried about that for the rest of the day because really, when all was said and done, Aidan hadn't been obliged to take over as her trainer. He'd said he'd done it to help Henry out of a predicament, but the fact remained that he could have said no, because in the end the only one who stood to gain from the arrangement was Lindsay herself. Later, however, when she tried to raise the matter with Aidan he looked at her as if she were mad.

'I don't know what you're talking about,' he said, his expression blank.

'This morning...' She swallowed. 'When you came into the staffroom...'

'Yes?' The blank expression was replaced by a frown.

'I was talking to Judith and you may have overheard something...'

'About whom?' The blue eyes were like ice chips again.

'Well, about you, actually.'

'So you and Judith were discussing me over your coffee?'

'No,' she said hastily. 'Not really... It's just that you may have thought...it may have sounded as if I was being ungrateful...'

'About what?'

'The fact that you've taken over the job of being my trainer. And I'm not ungrateful...really, I'm not...'

'Well, that's all right, then, isn't it?' The bland expression was back on his face.

'So…' She hesitated, uncertain of her ground now. 'Had you overheard?'

'No.' With a shrug he strode off through Reception, leaving Lindsay feeling decidedly foolish at offering explanations, even apologies, where none had been necessary.

She liked Judith Havers, a plain-speaking, down-to-earth Welsh girl who treated everyone as she found them and took no nonsense from anyone, including Bronwen. 'She thinks she's queen bee around here,' she told Lindsay when the pair of them were in the treatment room one afternoon, awaiting the first patients in a baby clinic. 'There's one of her kind in every practice—but she cuts no ice with me, I can tell you.'

'I just wish Gwynneth could take your attitude,' Lindsay replied. 'Bronwen practically terrorises her.'

'Poor little Gwynneth,' said Judith. 'She's not had a very good life so far. Her childhood was unhappy and she suffers from low self-esteem. Bronwen, on the other hand, is a bully and Gwynneth a natural victim.'

'I'm going to see if I can't change that situation around a little during my time here,' Lindsay replied thoughtfully.

'It would be good if you could,' Judith said. 'But be careful, it could make Bronwen even worse.'

'I know.' Lindsay nodded. 'That's what I'm afraid of. But there's nothing to stop me taking a bit of interest in Gwynneth.'

It wasn't difficult to please Gwynneth as the girl was so interested in Lindsay and constantly asked questions about her life in London.

'Were you in London on Millennium Eve?' she

asked one evening when they were in Reception, clearing up after a long, busy day.

'Yes,' Lindsay replied, glancing up from the repeat prescriptions she was signing. Bronwen was shutting down the computers for the night, and Aidan was standing with his back to them, reading some notes. Henry was still in his consulting room.

'Oh, I bet that was wonderful, wasn't it?' Gwynneth sighed.

'It was pretty impressive,' Lindsay agreed.

'So where were you?' Gwynneth persisted. 'Were you at the Dome?'

'No, I wasn't at the Dome. I had a meal with...with friends in a restaurant, then we went to someone's apartment overlooking the Thames to watch the fireworks.' She was suddenly aware that Bronwen was listening and that Aidan, even though he hadn't moved a muscle and still had his back to her, was also listening to every word of this conversation.

'So did you see that River of Fire and the Ferris wheel and all that?' breathed Gwynneth, her eyes like saucers.

'Yes, yes, I did...'

'Oh, that must have been really exciting.'

'Yes, it was.' Lindsay nodded. 'A moment in history.'

'A waste of money if you ask me.' Bronwen, who clearly *had* been listening, looked up from the computer. 'All that money going up in smoke all over the world. I'm sure it could have been put to much better use.'

'Yes, Bronwen, you're probably right,' Lindsay agreed. 'But I agree with Gwynneth. It was a one-off—none of us will never see the likes of it again.'

Aidan turned at that moment and Gwynneth flushed with pleasure that for once someone seemed to be agreeing with her. At the same moment the door of Henry's consulting room opened and Henry himself walked out into Reception, putting paid to any further idle chatter. Bronwen got on with the job of shutting down the computers, Gwynneth carried on filing the last of the day's records and Lindsay signed the final prescriptions.

It was only later when the two receptionists had left for home and Henry had said goodnight that Aidan spoke to her. He'd returned to his room after the conversation in Reception but he came out as Lindsay was about to go upstairs to her flat.

'That was kind,' he said abruptly.

She paused with one hand on the newel post and looked at him. 'What was?' she said blankly.

'Taking Gwynneth's part like that.'

'I only said what I felt.'

'Nevertheless, her opinions always seem to get crushed by Bronwen—it must have been a boost to her to have you agree with her.'

Lindsay gave a little shrug. 'I hate to see someone continually trodden on,' she said.

'I'm not even sure that Bronwen is aware that she does it. I think it's just become second nature to her to put Gwynneth down.'

'I don't think Bronwen can be a very happy person.'

'You may well be right.' He shrugged. 'I wouldn't know.'

He'd gone then, pulling up the collar of his waxed jacket and hunching his shoulders against the rain as he set off across the car park, leaving Lindsay to lock the door.

It was only later when she was preparing a meal that she found herself reflecting on what he'd said. It was rare to get praise from Aidan in any shape or form and she still wasn't exactly sure that had been what he'd given her when he'd commented on her taking Gwynneth's part. But at least, for once, he'd seemingly recognised Gwynneth's plight and that in itself couldn't be a bad thing.

The practice had hired a four-wheel-drive Jeep for Lindsay and while at first she thought she would miss driving her sports car, after a time she found she enjoyed driving the bigger vehicle, which was certainly more suited to the roads in the area. Within a comparatively short space of time her beloved sports car was fated to spend most of its time in the garage at the rear of the surgery.

As the area grew more familiar to her Lindsay appreciated its beauty even more than she had on her arrival. Sometimes on her days off she ventured farther afield—to Caenarvon through the dramatic Llanberis pass, to Conway and Rhyl and once she even crossed the Menaii bridge to the island of Anglesea. The dramatic and sometimes wild countryside, with its soaring mountains, tumbling waterfalls, rugged passes and deep wooded valleys, seemed to act as a kind of antidote to her pain at losing Andrew, and to her surprise in a fairly short space of time she found he actually occupied very little of her thoughts.

Towards the end of Lindsay's first month in Tregadfan the promised influx of tourists began to arrive. At first just a trickle and then a steady stream of caravans and motor homes, cyclists, hikers and climbers converged on Snowdonia.

At last Lindsay began to take surgeries on her own, even though she was required to report to Aidan on a daily basis. These surgeries were mainly made up of temporary residents and the overflow of the local surgeries. House calls she still attended with Aidan but she knew the day was rapidly approaching when she would be drawn into the on-call rota to take her turn.

One morning she'd just finished her surgery and, instead of reporting to Aidan as she usually did, he came to her consulting room. She looked up in surprise as he came into the room.

'How did it go?' he asked.

'All right.' She nodded and began leafing through the little stack of temporary resident forms which had made up the bulk of her surgery. 'Mostly predictable. A child with earache, another with mosquito bites. A man with a badly sprained ankle. A woman who'd left her medication at home—'

'What did she want?' Aidan had strolled to the French doors as she'd been speaking and was staring out into the conservatory.

'Nifedipine for high blood pressure, ranitidine for indigestion and ibuprofen for arthritic pain. I checked her blood pressure and asked her about the nature of her indigestion and how long she'd been taking the ibuprofen.'

'Did you think the two were connected in any way?'

'I don't think so. I know that non-steroidal anti-inflammatory drugs for arthritis can cause stomach bleeding and abdominal discomfort, but this patient's indigestion took the form of acidity and was intermittent, more in keeping with what she'd been eating. She admitted that since leaving home she'd been eating food she's unfamiliar with. Her own GP had prescribed the ranitidine on several previous occasions.'

'That's OK.' Aidan nodded. 'You have to be careful because sometimes a temporary resident will try it on. We had one once who'd gone to every practice in the area, saying he'd left his diazepam at home. He'd obtained quite a substantial amount before one of the local chemists spotted what was happening and alerted us.' He paused. 'What else did you have?'

'A baby with severe colic, a couple of cases of diarrhoea and vomiting and a child with a wooden splinter deeply embedded in her foot. I removed the splinter, gave a tetanus booster and sent her to Judith for a dressing.'

'The D-and-V cases—were they from the camping site?'

'I'm not sure. Just a minute.' She began leafing through the forms again. 'Yes. Yes, they were,' she admitted after a moment.

Aidan turned round and looked at her. 'From the same family?'

'Yes. The grandmother and one of the grandchildren.'

'That suggests it may have been something they've eaten in their own caravan. Let's hope so, otherwise we could be looking at an epidemic. Nothing like it over a weekend. Now, tell me, I know it's officially your afternoon off, but I have a call to go to a farm over on the far side of Capel Curig. Would you like to come with me?'

She knew he expected her to agree. 'Yes.' She nodded. 'Of course.'

'It's an interesting family,' he went on. 'They've had

a rough time recently. Mother is expecting her fourth child and father had an accident a couple of months ago—a disagreement with a particularly lethal piece of farm machinery. He's out of hospital now but life is far from easy. Her pregnancy is proving to be difficult and one of the children has severe asthma and eczema. I said I'd go over to take a look at them all.'

It was late afternoon by the time they were finally able to leave the surgery, but the early summer sun still felt warm on Lindsay's shoulders as she took her place beside Aidan in his Land Rover. He'd already collected the dogs and they both whined an ecstatic welcome. Lindsay had got used to the two of them by this time and actually found she was as pleased to see them as they obviously were to see her.

The hedgerows on either side of the roads as they left the village were thick with the blossom of the blackthorn, while in the meadows early scarlet poppies turned their faces to the sun and white daisies gathered in clusters like drifts of snowflakes.

With a little sigh Lindsay wound down her window and rested her arm on the sill. Already since she'd come to Tregadfan the sun had touched her skin in a different way from that of the fiercer Mediterranean sun, and a light dusting of freckles covered her nose. She'd abandoned the formality of her suits and blouses, opting instead for the more casual clothes she'd bought locally and which were so much more practical for the type of life she was now living. For their visit to the farm she was wearing a blue-and-white checked shirt, sleeves turned back to the elbow, tucked into a cream pair of twill trousers and secured with a leather belt. Her hair she wore loose instead of neatly secured by a scarf or slide, and as they trundled along the country roads it was caught by the wind. As it streamed behind her she closed her eyes and dreamily let her thoughts drift.

'Did I wake you?'

She opened her eyes and looked at Aidan. 'Sorry?' she said.

'I asked if I'd woken you.'

'I wasn't asleep,' she replied.

'You could have fooled me.' He gave an unexpected chuckle. 'On the other hand, maybe you just aren't speaking to me.'

'What do you mean?' she asked uncertainly.

'Well, I've been talking to you for the last five minutes and you don't appear to have heard a word I've been saying.'

Lindsay turned her head and looked out of the window. To her surprise she saw that they were high on a mountain road. 'I guess I must have drifted off for a while,' she mumbled.

'That's OK,' he said easily. 'It's nice to know you're so relaxed—or maybe its because we're working you too hard and you're simply dog-tired?'

'No,' she said quickly, hating the thought that he might think she couldn't cope. 'Of course not. I think it's all this fresh mountain air that's making me feel relaxed.'

'Well, I'm glad. You seemed very uptight when you first arrived.'

'That's hardly surprising,' she replied. 'After all, nothing was what I expected.'

'That's true,' he admitted. He paused then threw her a sidelong look. 'There's something that intrigues me,' he said.

'What's that?' she asked warily.

'A few months ago Henry said there was some doubt about whether you would be coming—in fact, he rather seemed to think it was all off. That was before Megan's illness, of course, and then quite suddenly it was all on again. I just wondered why, what happened so suddenly to make you change your mind.'

It was her turn to glance sideways at him. Aidan's expression was set as he concentrated on the winding road ahead, the rugged features taut, the startling blue eyes slightly narrowed. He, too, wore an open-necked shirt with the sleeves turned back, together with his olive-green chinos. The dark, reddish-brown hair, ruffled by the breeze, curled crisply above his ears and along the collar of his shirt.

Her first reaction was not to answer him. Why should she? It was none of his business why she'd nearly cancelled her year in North Wales then had suddenly changed her mind. There was nothing in her contract that said she had to tell him every detail of her life, even if he was her trainer. Then she slumped slightly. Why shouldn't she tell him? It didn't matter now. None of it mattered any more.

'I was in a relationship,' she said quietly. 'Then it ended.'

'Ah,' he replied. 'I thought it might be something like that.' He paused. 'Do you want to talk about it?'

'No,' she replied firmly. 'Absolutely not.'

# CHAPTER EIGHT

'HIS name was Andrew. He was a solicitor and we met through mutual friends.' They'd pulled into a lay-by, which they were now sharing with a couple of sheep. Behind them water cascaded from an outcrop of black rocks while before them the road twisted away into a deep valley, its sides covered in dense pines. In spite of Lindsay's resolve of only moments ago to tell Aidan nothing, it now all came pouring out. While the dogs dozed in the back he listened in silence.

'I thought it was for real,' she admitted quietly, 'and he seemed as smitten as I was. We'd only been dating for a short while when, quite by chance, I saw him in a restaurant. He was with a very attractive young woman and I knew he hadn't seen me. I decided to say nothing and see if he told me. I confided in my best friend, Annabelle, who tried to make me get the whole thing in perspective—you know, maybe she was a client or a colleague, that it was a business lunch, that sort of thing, and to remember that, after all, we hadn't made any real commitment to each other at that stage.'

'And *did* he tell you?' asked Aidan.

'No.' She shook her head. 'And somehow I couldn't quite bring myself to confront him with it. I didn't want to appear too possessive, especially at that point in the relationship, and I would have looked silly if it had simply been a client or a colleague. He also probably would have asked why I hadn't gone over to their table...and I...I couldn't answer that.'

They were silent for a while and Aidan simply waited without prompting her in any way. When Lindsay started to speak again Jess suddenly lifted her head and, seeing the sheep outside the Land Rover, gave a short, sharp bark. The sheep skittered away in fright, jostling and pushing each other as they went.

'If it had been just that it would hardly have mattered,' Lindsay went on at last as Jess settled down again. 'We carried on dating—had a wonderful time, really—then Andrew moved in with me. We'd talked of marriage but we both felt it was a little too soon for that. I was very happy with the situation and I felt fairly certain that marriage would eventually follow, then later we'd start a family, which we'd both said we wanted.'

She fell silent again and this time Aidan did break the silence. 'Something obviously happened to shatter this idyll,' he said. 'Unless, of course, you simply drifted apart or realised you'd made a mistake.'

'No.' She shook her head. 'You were right the first time…something happened. I overheard a conversation during an outpatients clinic at the hospital where I was working. A patient was being attended to in the cubicle next to the one where I was carrying out an examination. She obviously knew the nurse who was treating her and was telling her all about her new boyfriend. I didn't take much notice at first until I heard her mention the law firm where Andrew worked. As she carried on I gradually became aware that it was Andrew she was talking about.'

She paused and swallowed then after a moment continued, 'At first I thought I must be mistaken or that maybe there was someone else called Andrew who perhaps worked for the same firm, but the patient went on to mention other names and details which left me in no further doubt that it was my Andrew and that he was two-timing me.'

'I couldn't ignore it this time,' she went on after a moment. 'I confronted him with it. He tried to deny it and bluff his way out but I knew he was lying. I asked him to leave the flat immediately.' To her horror, as she finished speaking Lindsay felt tears spring to her eyes.

'Was that what affected your decision to come here?'

She nodded and the tears spilled over and rolled down her cheeks. Helplessly she dashed them away with the back of her hand. 'I'd decided some time ago, long before I met Andrew, that I wanted to come to Henry for my GP training, but when Andrew moved in with me I put the whole idea on hold and carried on with my work at the hospital. I hadn't decided what I would do in the long run but after Andrew moved out I went back to my original plan.'

Aidan was silent then, reaching out, he covered her hand with one of his. If anyone had prewarned her that that was what he would do she would have imagined she would snatch her hand away. But she didn't. She allowed her hand to remain beneath his where for a moment it felt warm and safe. 'And how do you feel now?' he asked quietly at last. 'Are you over him?'

'I wasn't when I first arrived, hence the tension that you noticed...' she said slowly.

'And now?' Aidan took his hand from hers and turned slightly in his seat so that he was half facing her.

Lindsay allowed herself to meet that unswerving blue gaze. 'I have to say I'm feeling better,' she admitted at last. 'Maybe not over it completely but, yes, well on the way, I think.'

'You sound surprised.' The hint of a smile played around his mouth.

'I am if I'm honest. There was a point when I thought I would never get over him—it's terribly hard, you know, when you've made a commitment to someone and then they betray you—but I have to say that, since coming here into a completely different way of life, I've had very little time to think about any aspect of my life in London, let alone Andrew.' She hesitated. 'I know,' she said after a moment, 'that it's hard to understand about betrayal and all that—I think only someone who has been there can truly understand.'

'Maybe I understand better than you think,' Aidan replied softly.

She stared at him. 'Are you saying you've been there?' she said curiously.

'Maybe.' He gave a slight shrug. 'But I think one of us unburdening is quite enough for one day. Besides, we need to get on if we're to make this visit.'

Leaning forward, he turned the key in the ignition and moments later they'd left the lay-by and were descending into the cool greenness of the valley. In places rapier-sharp rays of sunlight penetrated the darkness of the pines, illuminating the lighter green of sycamores or mountain ash and highlighting clumps of fresh green ferns amongst last year's dead bracken.

They travelled in silence but this time it was a peaceful silence and Lindsay found herself feeling relieved that she'd told him about the problems that had beset her when she'd arrived in Tregadfan. There had been a sense of understanding about him which, together with the allusion of shared experience, led her to believe that he, too, had indeed suffered as she had.

The farm was situated in a natural fold of land tucked in against the hillside, and as they approached down a rutted track at first sight the place appeared deserted. Countless sheep dotted the hills but the pens and outbuildings around the farm had an air of neglect about them. The house itself looked shabby and run-down and badly in need of a coat of paint. A line of washing stirred gently in the breeze at one side of the house, and as Aidan brought the Land Rover to a halt a gaggle of geese appeared from the direction of the barn and waddled by, gossiping noisily to each other as they went.

'Geese are such fascinating creatures,' said Lindsay as she climbed from the Land Rover, watching the little group until it disappeared from their sight.

'Maybe.' Aidan pulled a face. 'But they're also incredibly noisy.' At that moment a teenage youth came from one of the outbuildings and ambled across the yard towards them. 'Hello, Rufus.' Aidan nodded. 'Where's your mum?'

'She's indoors.' The boy jerked his head in the direction of the house.

'Thanks.' Aidan led the way to the house and rapped on the front door. After a long wait the door was opened by a small girl with dark, tangled hair wearing a grubby gingham dress that looked several sizes too big for her. Her face and arms were blotched with the red scaly patches of eczema. She stared at them then turned and shouted. 'Mum, it's the doctor.'

'Well, ask him in, then, silly child.' A woman appeared behind the little girl who continued to gape at Aidan and Lindsay. The woman was heavily pregnant and looked pale, drawn and very tired. 'Hello, Doctor,' she said. 'Come in—you mustn't mind Evie. And you won't have to mind the mess either,' she added as she led the way into a narrow hallway then into an incredibly cluttered living room.

'We haven't come to see your mess, Clarrie,' said Aidan. 'We've come to see you—and Dai. This is Dr Henderson, by the way.' He glanced over his shoulder at Lindsay. 'She's come to join us at the practice for a while.'

Clarrie Williams nodded at Lindsay. 'Nice to meet you,' she said wearily. Then turning, she said, 'Here's Dai now.' Supported by elbow crutches, a man came hobbling into the room. He was probably only around forty years of age but he looked ten years older. He nodded briefly at Aidan and threw Lindsay a curious look.

'How's it going, Dai?' Aidan cleared a space on the table and set down his case.

'Slow,' grunted Dai Williams. 'Too bloody slow. My farm's going to rack and ruin. I need to get back to work. Ted can't manage on his own and Rufus is bloody useless.'

'He's only a boy,' protested Clarrie. 'Anyway, I'll be back out there soon.'

'How's the leg?' asked Aidan.

'Painful,' Dai replied. 'I swear that pin is doing more harm than good.'

'Let's take a look at it,' said Aidan. Turning to Lindsay, who was hovering uncertainly near the doorway, he said, 'While I'm looking at Dai's leg, Lindsay, how about you check up on Clarrie? Here are her notes.'

'All right.' Lindsay was pleased to be given something to do. She was beginning to feel quite claustro-

phobic in this household. 'Could we go up to the bedroom, do you think?' she asked Clarrie hopefully as
she took the record envelope that Aidan handed to her.

'If you like.' Clarrie shrugged. 'It's in a mess up
there as well.' Slowly she led the way back into the
hall and up the steep staircase. 'You here for good?'
she asked over her shoulder as they neared the top.

'Oh, no,' Lindsay replied. 'Only for a year then I'll
be going home.'

'Where's that?' Clarrie pushed open a door and
stood back for Lindsay to enter the bedroom.

'London.'

'London, eh?' Clarrie gave a tired smile. 'You must
find it a bit different round here, then.'

'Just a bit,' Lindsay replied with a grin. 'Do you
know London at all?'

'I had a holiday there when I was a girl—in another
lifetime.' The ghost of a smile flickered over Clarrie's
features. 'There was this lad I met, you see—down at
the camp site in Tregadfan. I worked there a couple of
seasons when I was still at school. He lived in London,
well, Peckham. I stayed with him and his family.'

'I take it this was in pre-Dai days?' asked Lindsay
as she opened her case while Clarrie sat on the bed and
awkwardly lay back against the pillows.

'Sort of. Although I've always known Dai. We grew
up together.' Clarrie shrugged but she didn't elaborate
any further about what had happened to the boy from
Peckham.

'Now, let's see, how many weeks are you?' Lindsay
glanced at Clarrie's notes.

'Thirty-seven,' Clarrie replied. 'And I'll be glad
when it's all over, I can tell you. I've been more tired
with this one than with the other three put together.'

'Well, you've got all the others to cope with this time and it doesn't sound to me as if things are particularly easy at the moment.'

'You can say that again.' Clarrie pulled a face. 'And I sometimes think Dai is worse than the kids. He's been like a caged animal since his accident—anyone would think it was my fault the way he goes on about it. Trouble is, the bills are piling up. Things were bad even before Dai's accident. Now, well...' she gave a hopeless little gesture with her hands '...I can just see the whole lot going down the pan, the farm and everything.'

'Let's hope it won't come to that,' said Lindsay. 'But for the moment the most important thing has to be you and your baby. Tell me, are you going for a hospital delivery?'

'No.' Clarrie shook her head. 'I had the others at home. It'll be the same for this one.'

'I was just thinking that a spell in hospital, however brief, might just give you the break you need.'

Clarrie shook her head. 'No,' she said. 'It's all arranged. The district midwife will come in for the birth then my sister will help out for a couple of days or so—if she doesn't fall out with Dai.'

'Let's just check your blood pressure and listen to baby's heartbeat.' Lindsay perched on the side of the bed and applied the cuff to Clarrie's arm.

'It's a bit on the high side,' she said when she'd finished. 'You must get as much rest as you can. I know that's probably easier said than done,' she added when a sound like a snort came from Clarrie. 'But you must try. Would you like me to have a word with Dai?'

Clarrie shrugged. 'Can if you like. I doubt it would make much difference.' Raising herself onto her elbows, she watched Lindsay who was listening to the foetal heartbeat. 'Is everything all right?' There was a touch of anxiety in her voice now.

'Yes.' Lindsay straightened up. 'A nice strong heartbeat. What do you want this time, a boy or a girl?'

'Don't mind really.' Clarrie rearranged her clothing and sat up. 'Although I suppose another girl would even things up.'

'So you have Rufus and Evie and...?'

'Jared—he's twelve. Rufus is sixteen and Evie is six. I thought I'd finished,' she said ruefully. 'Just shows how wrong you can be, doesn't it?'

'I understand Evie suffers from asthma and eczema?' Lindsay began putting her stethoscope and the sphygmomanometer back into her case.

'Yes, it's been bad again just recently.' Clarrie rose to her feet and immediately sank back down onto the bed again. 'Oh,' she gasped. 'I feel giddy. I must have got up too quickly.'

'Rest for a moment,' said Lindsay.

Clarrie was silent for a while then she looked up. 'Where were we?' she said. 'Oh, yes, Evie. She's been coughing a lot just lately. Trouble is, she *will* handle the animals and her eczema has flared up again.'

'I'm sure Dr Lennox will be taking a look at her,' said Lindsay. 'But if he's still busy with your husband then I will.'

'He's nice, Dr Lennox,' said Clarrie as she once again attempted to get to her feet, more slowly this time. 'We used to have old Dr Meredith. He was OK but he could be quite blunt. I can remember him and Dai having words on more than one occasion. Dr Lennox is different.'

'I think he could stand his ground if the need arose,' said Lindsay.

'Oh, I don't doubt it.' Clarrie nodded, then with a little frown she said, 'Why are you going around with him?'

'He's my trainer. Oh, don't worry,' she added when she saw Clarrie's look of surprise, 'I am a doctor, but I have to find out what it takes to be a GP.'

'So you and he are spending quite a bit of time together.'

'You could say that.' Lindsay laughed. 'In fact, you could say I'm his shadow at the moment.'

'And how does Bronwen like that?'

It was Lindsay's turn to look surprised. 'You know Bronwen?' she said.

'Oh, yes.' Clarrie nodded. 'She lives next door to my sister.'

'I'd forgotten how close this community is. I suppose I assumed that because you live up here that you have little communication with those down in Tregadfan.'

'You'd be surprised.' Clarrie gave a short laugh. 'My sister has told me all about Bronwen and Dr Lennox.'

'What about them?' Lindsay grew very still. Was there something between Bronwen and Aidan after all? Had her earlier hunch been correct, unlikely as it had seemed? 'Is there something between them?' she asked at last.

'Oh, I don't know about that,' Clarrie replied. 'I would put it down to no more than wishful thinking on Bronwen's part.'

So was that all it was? thought Lindsay as she followed Clarrie downstairs, Bronwen wishing there could be something between Aidan and herself, or could it

be that there actually was? Aidan had hinted earlier that
he'd known what it was to be betrayed by someone—
but that could hardly be Bronwen, not if she was the
one wanting a relationship. Maybe she knew about the
one who had let him down and was simply offering
him a shoulder to cry on in the hope it could progress
into something more.

On the other hand, the whole thing could simply be
no more than village gossip, in which case it was best
left well alone. Not that it was any of her concern anyway. It really didn't matter to her what Aidan Lennox
did or didn't do in his private life, she told herself as
she and Clarrie joined Aidan in the living room. Here,
he'd finished examining Dai and had turned his attention to Evie.

'I'm going to change the dose of Evie's beclometh-
osone inhalers.' Aidan looked up at Clarrie. 'Also the
cream for her eczema—we'll try increasing the strength
for a while. If that doesn't work we'll have to see about
another course of steroids. You are still using the aque-
ous cream for washing, aren't you?'

Clarrie nodded. 'Yes. I can't think of anything we've
done differently lately or anything that could have
caused a reaction—apart from her handling the animals.'

'You must try not to, Evie,' said Aidan gently to the
little girl, who hung her head then buried her face in
her mother's lap. 'I know it's easier said than done on
a farm,' he went on, 'just as I know how much you
love animals'. He glanced up at Lindsay. 'Everything
all right?' he asked.

She knew he meant with Clarrie's pregnancy, and
when she nodded in reply he stood up and said, 'In

that case, we'll be going. I'll arrange the physiotherapy for you, Dai—you'll get an appointment.'

Dai merely grunted and it was Clarrie who saw them to the door. 'Thank you both,' she said.

'Will you be able to get the prescriptions?' asked Lindsay anxiously.

Clarrie nodded. 'Yes, Ted, who works for us on the farm, will collect them for us when he goes down to Betws-y-coed for supplies.'

'Look after yourself, Clarrie,' said Aidan.

'Yes,' said Lindsay, 'and try to get some rest.'

Moments later they were in the Land Rover and he was driving out of the farmyard. Lindsay glanced back as they turned into the lane and saw that Clarrie was still standing in the open doorway, watching them, with Evie by her side. Just before they moved out of sight of the farmhouse the geese returned, indignantly flapping and waddling around the side of the house to investigate the disturbance from the noise of the Land Rover's engine.

'It's another world,' said Lindsay as, with a little sigh, she settled back into her seat. 'It's amazing to me that people live out their entire lives in these remote hillside farms, just tending their sheep.'

'Usually most of them are quite happy to do so,' Aidan replied. 'Sometimes the youngsters will attend college, often agricultural college, then they'll go away for a while. But more often than not, a boy will return and take over running the family farm.'

'And the girls?'

'Nine times out of ten they'll end up marrying a farmer—usually someone they've known all their lives.'

'Like Clarrie,' said Lindsay. 'That's what happened

to her. She told me she and Dai were at school to-gether.'

Aidan nodded. 'That's right, they were.'

'They don't seem very happy.'

'What's happened to them is unfortunate. Farming has been hit very badly just lately and that alone is a big enough worry, but for Dai to have an accident as well which has put him out of action...' Aidan trailed off but his words implied his doubts that the family would ever recover.

They travelled in silence for a while then Aidan spoke again. 'Was Clarrie all right?'

'Her blood pressure was a bit on the high side, her ankles were swollen and she's very tired, but the foetal heartbeat was strong. I urged her to rest as much as she could.'

'That'll be easier said than done in the present circumstances.'

'I know.' Lindsay sighed. 'Are you happy with her having a home confinement?' she added curiously.

'It would be extremely difficult talking someone like Clarrie into a hospital confinement, but, I agree, the situation being what it is, she would certainly benefit from one.'

'Could we not have a word with the district mid-wife?'

'We could try. But I warn you, she'll be firmly on Clarrie's side. It's a sort of culture amongst these people to have their children in their own homes and the midwives themselves are proud of their births.'

'How will Dai get down for his physiotherapy?'

'Heaven knows.' Aidan shrugged. 'I hope Ted will be able to take him in the truck, but I doubt he'll have the time. Poor chap is hard-pressed enough as it is. In the end, I don't suppose Dai will go.'

'The boy, Rufus—shouldn't he be at school?' asked Lindsay.

'Probably—but he left at Easter when he was sixteen so that he could help Ted on the farm.'

'It really is a desperate situation, isn't it?'

'I told you it was, didn't I? Trouble is, I can't see it getting a lot better.'

'But surely after Carrie has had the baby and Dai is better…' She trailed off, threw Aidan a quick glance and when he didn't reply she said, 'Dai will *get* better, won't he?'

'Well, I certainly hope he'll get better than he is at the moment, but that leg is taking a long time to heal and there's tendon damage in his right arm. I have to confess there are times when I simply can't see him running a farm again.'

'What would they do?'

'Their only option would be to sell up. Trouble is, in the present climate they wouldn't get a lot for the farm. When I suggested it to Dai shortly after his accident he almost bit my head off. He's a very proud man. The farm was passed down to him by his father and he sees it as his duty to pass it on to Rufus.'

By the time they reached Tregadfan the sun was setting and dusk was beginning to steal its way across the mountains and into the valleys, and Lindsay had quite forgotten that she'd given up her time off to accompany Aidan. She felt it had been time well spent, for not only had she gained further insight into the people of the community she had come to work amongst, but also—probably because she'd chosen to confide in him—she and Aidan for the first time had reached a deeper level of understanding.

# CHAPTER NINE

'I'LL give some Lomotil for the diarrhoea and Maxolon for the sickness.' It was very cramped inside the tent and Lindsay was forced to kneel on the ground to write out the prescription. 'And I should stick to bottled water and maybe just a plain biscuit for a while,' she added to the white-faced young man lying in his sleeping bag.

'When will he be all right to go climbing?' asked his companion anxiously. 'We've got lots of expeditions planned.'

As the man on the ground groaned Lindsay looked up. 'Well, I shouldn't think he'll feel much like climbing for a couple of days or so. How long are you here for?'

'A week.'

'In that case, I would think he'll be feeling well enough to join you a bit later in the week.' She looked down at the patient. 'But for the time being you need to stay here and rest. You'll be quite weak for a time. I'll leave a few of these sachets.'

'What are they?' The second youth took the sachets Lindsay handed to him.

'Dioralyte,' Lindsay replied. 'It's a glucose-based product, which will help to replace the fluids he's lost and build up his strength again—that's essential after any kind of stomach bug.'

'OK, and thanks, Doc. Thanks for coming out. He was too weak to move.'

'That's all right,' Lindsay nodded. 'Keep an eye on him.' Lifting the tent flap, she scrambled out into the field at the back of the caravan park which was reserved for tents.

It was a week after her and Aidan's visit to the farm outside Capel Curig, and Lindsay's first Sunday on call on her own.

'Do you think you're ready for it?' Henry had sounded anxious when she'd told him about it.

'I think so.' She'd nodded.

'She knows where we are if she hits any tricky patches,' Aidan had said. 'I shan't be going far from home and I doubt you will either, Henry.'

'Henry had shaken his head. 'You're right. Although...' he'd paused and the other two had looked at him '...I have to say Megan has seemed a little better in the last few days. I'm almost afraid to say it in case I go home and find her exhausted again, but I'd thought that if it lasts over the weekend I might try and take her out for a little run on Sunday.'

'That sounds marvellous,' Lindsay had said.

'A change of scenery could work wonders,' Aidan had replied. 'Just as long as you're prepared that the improvement will probably not last, given the nature of ME.'

Henry had nodded. 'I know—we have to seize the moment, as they say.'

Lindsay didn't know whether the moment had lasted but as she drove out of the campsite she found herself fervently hoping that it had. A drive in the countryside on a sparkling summer's day such as this would surely only do Megan good.

So far she was managing her day on call very well. Already she'd coped with a child in the village suffering from severe stomach pains. She'd diagnosed appendicitis and had had the child transferred to hospital. She'd visited a couple of elderly patients, one with terminal cancer who was awaiting the community nurse to give him his morphine injection and another who needed oxygen for a chronic respiratory condition.

On the way back to the village from the campsite, on a sudden impulse Lindsay decided to call in on Douglas and Milly.

After parking the Jeep in front of the cottage, she opened the gate and walked up the path. The flower-beds on either side were packed with summer flowers, from polyanthus and pansies in the front of the border to delphiniums and hollyhocks against the wooden fence that divided the garden from the next-door cottage. Lindsay stood at the front door, after ringing the bell, and watched as a bee hovered over a pot of marigolds on the doorstep. To the right of the door on the crazy-paving pathway leading to the rear of the cottage a thrush was trying to crack a snail shell.

Lindsay was so taken by the bird's perseverance that it was some while before she realised that not only had no one come to answer the door but that there was no sound from within the cottage. She rang the bell again, and when faced with the same silence she made her way round to the back garden.

There was a lean-to beside the back door and as Lindsay rounded the side of the house she could see that the door was open. Probably Milly was in the back garden and simply hadn't heard the bell.

There was no sign of her, however, and in the end Lindsay tapped on the open door and called out. Still there was no reply, and then from within the cottage she heard a thumping noise. Uneasy now, she pushed the door fully open.

'Hello,' she called. 'Milly, are you there?'

When the thumping grew louder and somehow more persistent Lindsay entered the cottage and made her way through the tiny, neat kitchen.

Something was wrong, she knew there was, and as she left the kitchen her fears were confirmed as she tried to open the living-room door and found she could only open it a couple of inches because something was wedged behind it. With a muttered exclamation she tried to push the door, and when she found it was impossible she ran back through the cottage into the garden and round to the living-room window. With her hands around her eyes to block the light of the sun, she peered through the window.

Milly was lying on the floor against the door and Doug was sitting in his usual chair. He was holding his Zimmer frame which he was banging on the floor. That had been the thumping noise Lindsay had heard and which he was obviously doing to try to attract attention.

She knocked loudly on the window but it was with extreme difficulty that Doug slowly turned and saw her. Lindsay immediately realised that this must be one of his bad days and that there was no way that he could get up to open the window. For a split second her reaction was to call Aidan on her mobile phone then she dismissed it. This was her problem. She was the doctor on call—she must be the one to assess the situation and to cope with it.

Taking her mobile from her pocket, she dialled for an ambulance, giving brief details of the situation. Afterwards she looked around for something with which to break the window. The border of the crazy-paving pathway had an edging of broken tiles and, kneeling down, she prised one of these out of the ground. She hesitated for only a moment before breaking the glass, but luckily the panes were quite small and she could see that if she broke the one nearest to the window-catch she should be able to put her hand inside and open the window.

The sound of breaking glass shattered the peace of the quiet Sunday morning and Lindsay barely had time to put her hand through the opening when there came a shout from the other side of the fence that divided the back gardens.

'Oi! Who's that?'

Lindsay turned and to her amazement saw Hew Griffiths peering over the top of the fence, his face red with indignation.

'Oh, Hew,' Lindsay gasped. 'Mr Griffiths—I'm so glad it's you. Do you live there?'

'Of course I do, and I want to know what the hell you think you're doing.'

'What?' By this time Lindsay had succeeded in opening the window. All that was required now was to hoist herself up and climb through. She glanced wildly over her shoulder at Hew. 'Milly has collapsed,' she said breathlessly.

'Well, wouldn't it be better to go through the door?' Quite obviously, from where he was standing Hew could see that the back door was open.

'Oh, no,' said Lindsay, thankful that she was wearing trousers and not one of her Kensington suits as she hoisted herself up onto the window-sill. 'You don't understand. Milly is on the floor behind the living-room door. I couldn't open it.'

'What about Douglas?' called Hew.

'He's here. Look, could you come round? I'll try and move Milly and open the door.'

Muttering to himself, Hew disappeared from sight while Lindsay jumped to the floor of the living room.

'It's…M-Milly,' Douglas managed to stutter.

'I know.' Lindsay reassuringly touched him on the shoulder as she hurried past his chair.

Milly was barely conscious, mumbling incoherently, her face contorted, a trail of saliva on her chin and her left arm hanging limply. 'Milly, it's Lindsay—Dr Henderson,' she said as she crouched beside the elderly woman and checked her pulse. 'I'm going to try and move you and make you more comfortable,' she went on, grabbing a couple of cushions from the settee. Carefully she eased Milly away from the door and put the cushions beneath her head. Milly had obviously been in the process of preparing Sunday lunch when she'd collapsed, because she was wearing a flowered pinafore over her skirt and cardigan. It also looked as if she'd brought Douglas his morning coffee, for beside him was a plate of oatcakes and a cup and saucer, its contents gone cold.

Milly began mumbling again and appeared to be getting agitated, and Lindsay knelt beside her. 'It's all right, Milly. Really it is,' she said. 'You're going to be fine. And Douglas. He's all right, too.'

At that moment there came a rattle at the handle of the living-room door. 'Is that you, Hew? Come in.' Lindsay looked up as Hew's head appeared round the door.

'What's happened?' Hew stood in the doorway, looking in disbelief from Milly to Douglas.

'Milly's had a stroke, Hew. I've called an ambulance. They're on their way. Now, would you go to the bedroom, please, and bring me a blanket from the bed.'

Still muttering to himself, Hew took himself off upstairs. Lindsay opened her case and took out her stethoscope and sphygmomanometer. Carefully she applied the stethoscope and listened to Milly's heartbeat. She was about to secure the cuff on her arm to check her blood pressure when Hew returned with a pink blanket.

'Thanks, Hew.' Lindsay took the blanket from him and tucked it around Milly. 'We must keep her warm. Now, would you go and talk to Douglas? See if there's anything he wants.'

'What are you doing?' Hew frowned.

'I'm just checking Milly's blood pressure,' Lindsay replied.

'You say the ambulance is coming?' said Hew after a moment.

'Yes.' Lindsay nodded. 'Milly will have to go to hospital.'

'What about Douglas? He can't stay on his own. She does everything for him.'

'Yes, I know. Do any of their family live nearby, Hew?'

'No.' He shook his head. 'Their son lives near Oxford and their daughter's abroad. Canada, I think, or is it New Zealand? One or the other.'

'In that case, I think I'll have a word with Sister on the medical ward and see what she suggests,' said Lindsay. Picking up her mobile again, she dialled the number of the hospital which was on intake that weekend. Once she was through to the ward she explained the situation to the sister, who said she thought the best thing would be for Douglas to be admitted as well as Milly then an assessment could be done by Social

Services to decide what course of action would be best for them both.

As she switched off her phone Lindsay moved across the room to Douglas and crouched down before him.

'Douglas,' she said gently, and when she was reasonably certain she had his attention, she went on, 'I've arranged for Milly to go to hospital.' Douglas began shaking uncontrollably. 'And you are going with her,' she added.

'It's all right, Doug, my old boyo,' said Hew. 'You'll be all right. And Milly's going to be just fine.'

At the mention of his wife's name Douglas moved his head and looked at her where she lay on the floor. Both Lindsay and Hew followed his gaze. Milly looked anything but fine and they all knew it.

Taking Douglas's hand Lindsay squeezed it reassuringly. 'I'll go and put a few things together for you both before the ambulance arrives,' she said. Turning to Hew, she added, 'Will you sit with them for a moment, Hew? I won't be long.'

Hew nodded. He looked stunned by the events of the morning, not at all like the man who'd taken none too kindly to Lindsay on their previous encounter in the surgery on Lindsay's first day in Tregadfan.

Lindsay slipped from the room and hurried upstairs, where she found nightclothes and toiletries for both Milly and Douglas and packed them into a holdall which she lifted down from the top of a wardrobe. When she'd finished she looked round the bedroom, which was as neat and immaculate as the rest of the cottage. She doubted whether either husband or wife would return to this place which had been their home for so many years. For a moment the sadness caught in her throat. As she descended the stairs she was thankful that the ambulance had just arrived and she had to hurry forward to let the paramedics in.

'Dr Henderson?'

'Yes, come in.' Lindsay stood back for the two men to enter the cottage. 'Mrs Morgan has had a CVA. Her pulse is faint but steady—she's semi-conscious.' She led the way into the living room. 'We also have a problem with her husband, who has Parkinson's. I've had a word with the duty sister on the medical ward and she's happy to admit them both.'

'*Both* of them?' The elder paramedic drew in his breath sharply. 'Our shout was for one.' He shook his head.

'Yes, I know it was originally,' Lindsay agreed. 'But I wasn't too certain about Mr Morgan then. I realise now that there's no way he can stay here on his own and there are no relatives nearby.'

The paramedic looked at Doug then turned and looked down at Milly. 'Well,' he said, scratching his head, 'we don't know about that, do we, Mark?' He glanced at the younger man who also shook his head. 'If we start doing things like that, they'll all want to start bringing their other halves in with them.'

For one awful moment Lindsay thought he was going to refuse, then he said, 'You're new here, aren't you, doc? Locum or trainee?'

'Trainee,' Lindsay replied. 'But...' She was about to explain yet again that she was fully qualified and well within her rights to admit anyone to hospital whom she deemed necessary when the man suddenly grinned. 'Don't look so worried, love. Course we'll take him. Won't we, Doug?'

'Oh,' said Lindsay in relief. 'Do you know him?'

'Know him? I should say so. Many's the time we've

taken Doug to Outpatients or to the day unit.' He crouched down beside Milly. 'Hello, Milly, my love,' he said. He spoke to her just as he would have at any other time. 'Now, what do you think you've been up to? I know, don't tell me. You were getting a bit fed up with Doug having all the attention, weren't you? Well, we'll soon sort that one out. Me and young Mark here are going to put you onto a stretcher, then we're going to take you out to the ambulance. After that, we'll come back and get Doug into a chair, then we'll take him out.' He glanced up at Lindsay. 'Her breathing's a bit laboured,' he said.

'Can you give her some oxygen?' asked Lindsay.

'Sure.' The older paramedic, whose name turned out to be Vincent, soon had an oxygen mask in place over Milly's face, and in a very short space of time she was being transported out to the waiting ambulance. Lindsay accompanied her, leaving Hew with Doug, then she stayed with Milly in the ambulance while the two paramedics went back for Doug.

At last both husband and wife were on their way to hospital, and with a little sigh Lindsay went back into the cottage.

'Don't you worry about nothing here, Doctor,' said Hew. 'I'll get that window boarded up and clear up the glass, then I'll lock up and take the keys in with me. My wife will be back soon—she's gone to chapel. She'll be wanting to go and see Milly.'

'I should give it a few days, Hew,' Lindsay replied. 'Milly won't be up to visitors for a while.'

'She was in a bad way, wasn't she, Doctor?' Hew frowned.

'Yes, Hew. I'm afraid she was.' Lindsay nodded

then picked up her case. 'Well, I must be going. I'm still on call. Thank you for your help here, Hew.'

'Don't mention it. I was glad to be of help. We've been neighbours for a long time.'

Hew saw her to the door and even raised his hand in a wave as she drove away. Lindsay couldn't help a smile. This was a far cry from the suspicious character she'd seen before. Maybe at last she was beginning to be accepted by the locals. Whatever, she was just thankful that her impulse had taken her to see the Morgans that morning. She doubted whether Milly would have survived too much longer without medical treatment.

It proved to be a day of sudden impulses because as she drove back towards the village Lindsay decided to call in at Aidan's cottage. He'd told her he would be around all day should she need any help. Far from needing his help, or even advice, she suddenly felt an urgent need to see him, even if it was only to tell him how well she'd coped in the crisis with Milly and Doug.

She parked the Jeep on the road and approached the cottage by way of the steps at the rear. This time the steps were dry and she was wearing her sensible walking shoes. She smiled to herself as she recalled the previous occasion when it had been raining heavily and she'd been wearing her black patent-leather shoes with the gold trim on the heels. It had been after that that Aidan had advised her to get herself some sensible footwear for country visits. That in turn had led to the argument about her going shopping without consulting him first. She had to admit that things had certainly improved between them since then.

Lindsay could hear a thudding noise as she de-

scended the steps, and for one moment she was reminded of Douglas thumping the floor with his frame
to attract attention to Milly's plight. This noise was
louder, more of a thud than a thump, and the last thing
she expected it to be was Aidan with a Zimmer frame.
It conjured up such an unlikely image that even the
thought of it made her smile.

When she reached the foot of the steps and turned
into the little courtyard at the side of his cottage she
had a clear view of the garden. Aidan was a short distance away and, clad in a thin T-shirt and jeans, was
wielding an axe, splitting logs on a block.

Beyond him the two dogs were lying on the ground,
their heads on their paws as they watched him. They
both saw Lindsay but so used to her were they by now
that they didn't even bother to bark. Skipper merely
raised his head in greeting and panted a little louder,
while Jess wagged her tail fervently.

Lindsay paused, watching Aidan, not wanting to dis-
turb him or interrupt the rhythm of the axe. With every
cycle, from him lifting the axe to a wide arc then bringing it down on one of the large logs he was splitting
into smaller pieces, the muscles across his back and
shoulders rippled and strained against the thin fabric of
his T-shirt. Sweat was seeping from beneath the dark
tangle of his hair and trickling down his forehead.
There was something raw, almost primeval about the
picture he presented, and deep inside Lindsay felt the
stirrings of a responding desire.

It wasn't until he stopped to change the position of
the log that he must have sensed that something was
different. Maybe it was to do with the attitude of the
dogs, maybe not, but, whatever it was, he turned suddenly and saw her watching him.

Their gazes met and it was as if the next moment were suspended in time. The breath caught in Lindsay's throat and she could have sworn that her heart stopped beating.

Then Aidan spoke and the moment, both sweet and painful, was over. She breathed again and was left with just a dull pain somewhere under her ribs, the memory of which would act as a brief reminder of that moment.

'I didn't know you were there,' he said quietly. Turning to the dogs, he added, 'Fine watchdogs you turned out to be.'

'They know me now,' said Lindsay in the dogs' defence. 'Instead of a bark I get panting and tail-wagging these days.'

Suddenly it seemed to dawn on Aidan that she may have had a reason for visiting him. 'Is there a problem?' he asked, his eyes narrowing slightly.

'No,' she said quickly. 'At least, there might have been but I think I've solved it. Anyway, I hope I have.'

'I was about to have a Coke,' he said, wiping his brow with the back of his arm. 'Would you care to join me? Then you can tell me all about it.'

'OK.' She tried to sound casual but for some reason her heart was still doing unpredictable things. After having apparently stopped during that one incredible moment, when time seemed to have stood still it had now started to pound uncomfortably.

'You've got your mobile with you?' asked Aidan, and when she nodded in response he disappeared into the cottage. Lindsay sat down on the edge of a large, upturned terracotta flower-tub and looked around her at the glorious wilderness that was his garden. It was very peaceful, the only sounds being the singing of grasshoppers from the undergrowth and the occasional hum of an engine as a car passed the cottage on the road above.

Lindsay rested her head against the wall and lifted her face to the sun as a kind of contentment stole over her. She hadn't felt this way for a long time, and if anyone had asked her to analyse her feelings she would have said she was happy, which in itself was surprising, given how she'd felt only a short while ago.

How had this happiness happened? How had it crept up on her without her being aware of it?

Surely it couldn't have anything to do with Aidan?

Opening her eyes, she saw that he had come out of the cottage and, with a glass of Coke in each hand, was crossing the courtyard towards her. Quite suddenly, she knew with profound certainty that her newly found sense of happiness had everything to do with Aidan.

# CHAPTER TEN

AIDAN handed Lindsay one of the glasses then perched on the edge of the low wall that separated the courtyard from the rest of the garden. Jess cocked one ear and lifted her head to see what was going on. Satisfied that all was well in the life of her master, she rested her head on her paws once more. Skipper was already snoring.

Aidan lifted his glass. 'Cheers,' he said.

'Cheers.' Lindsay joined him, taking a sip while he took a long draught of his drink.

'Ah,' he said in obvious satisfaction. 'I needed that—almost as good as a pint.'

'I'm surprised you haven't got a pint,' observed Lindsay.

'Can't take any chances,' he replied, setting his glass down on the flagstones. 'Never know if you might need some help when you're on call then I'd need to drive. Speaking of which...' He paused and threw her a side-long glance. 'You have something to tell me?'

'I have. And I'll doubt if you'll believe this.'

'Oh, I don't know, there's very little that surprises me in this game. That's one thing I have learnt over the years.'

'OK. So what would you say if I were to tell you that at this very moment both Douglas and Milly Morgan are in hospital?'

Aidan had picked up his glass again, but without as much as taking a sip he lowered it and stared at her.

133

'There you are,' she said. 'You are surprised, aren't you? I said you would be.'

'What happened?' The blue eyes had narrowed and the tone of his voice had changed.

Lindsay found herself nervously licking her lips and hated herself for it. She'd coped, hadn't she, for heaven's sake? So why should she feel nervous at explaining her actions? Aidan Lennox was why. And the fact that he was sitting there in the sunshine, looking incredibly sexy, didn't help either. But he was waiting, and the narrowed gaze had turned into a frown.

'Milly's had a stroke,' she said.

He continued to stare at her in the same disconcerting manner. 'So who called you in?' he said at last.

'Actually, no one called me in. It was the most incredible coincidence. I just happened to be passing— I'd been called up to the camping site and on my way back I thought I'd just look in—'

'What for?'

'What do you mean?' She frowned. This wasn't going as she'd hoped. She'd imagined he would be pleased that she'd decided to call on the Morgans at such an opportune moment, instead of which he seemed annoyed if his expression was anything to go by.

'Why did you feel the need to call in? Did you think you'd go in the hopes that Milly would offer you coffee and some of her oatcakes?'

'Of course not.' Lindsay felt the colour rush to her cheeks.

'So what, then?' he persisted.

'Just to see them. To see how they were.'

'A professional visit, then?'

'I suppose so. If you like.'

'But you know I do that. You know I call in each week to keep an eye on them.'

'Yes, I know you do.' Lindsay was holding onto her temper with difficulty now. 'But it was purely an impulse thing. And as it turned out, it was a jolly good job I did. If I hadn't, Milly would probably still be lying there on the floor—'

'Just a minute.' He cut her short again then, carefully setting his glass down once more, he went on, 'Now, let's get this straight. You called on the Morgans purely on impulse and you say Milly was on the floor? So whereabouts was this?'

'In the living room...'

'How did you get in?' he asked.

'I had to break a window.'

'You did what?' He stared at her incredulously.

'A window...I had to break one. But don't worry. Hew Griffiths—he lives next door to the Morgans—'

'I know where Hew Griffiths lives.' Aidan's voice was bleak now.

'Yes, well, he heard the sound of the glass breaking, and after I'd climbed through the window he came round. He's going to board up the window...so it'll be perfectly all right.'

'Did it not occur to you to contact the police before you started breaking into someone's home? Isn't that the usual procedure where you come from? Because it sure as hell is around here.' At the change of tone Jess lifted her head and gave a short, single bark.

Lindsay struggled to remain calm. 'I know the procedure. Of course I do. I'm not a student, Aidan.'

'So if you know the procedure why didn't you apply it in this case?'

'Because I didn't actually have to break in.'

'You said you smashed a window. That sounds like breaking in to me.'

'Well, it wasn't, actually.' By this time Lindsay could really feel her hackles rising as she sought to defend her actions. She took a deep breath, more to steady her nerves than anything else, then went on to explain exactly how she'd found Milly. 'I could see at once that she'd suffered a CVA,' she concluded at last.

'Was she conscious?' Aidan demanded.

'Barely.'

'So how long do you think it was since it happened?'

'Not too long. She'd brought Douglas his morning coffee but something had prevented him from drinking it. It had gone cold in the cup.'

'What time was this?'

'About eleven-thirty.'

'So she probably had the stroke just after ten-thirty. That's the time Milly makes morning coffee. What did you do next?'

'I moved Milly into a more comfortable position,' Lindsay replied. 'Hew had arrived by then. He sat with Douglas while I listened to Milly's heart and checked her blood pressure. There really wasn't anything else I could do except wait for the ambulance. Hew then pointed out that Douglas wouldn't be able to stay on his own because it was Milly who did everything for him.'

'Had that not occurred to you?'

'Well, yes, I knew that, of course, but I suppose I thought there might be family or someone who could help him, but when Hew said there was no one I decided to ring the medical ward and speak to the duty sister to see if Douglas could be admitted as well.'

'You did what?' Rising to his feet, Aidan glared down at her.

'What else was I to do?' she protested. 'I could hardly leave him there on his own. As it happened, the duty sister was very understanding and said she would admit him to the ward where he could be looked after until an assessment could be made sometime tomorrow.'

'That means Social Services will become involved and he'll be put into Rhondda House—'

'Yes, but you said yourself that was what would eventually happen, that Milly wouldn't be able to cope for much longer.'

'I'd promised Milly if the worst came to the worst I would try and get them both into the same home. Now Social Services are involved I can't see that happening... And once Douglas is in Rhondda House that's where he'll stay...'

'Maybe Milly will be able to go to Rhondda House eventually as well.'

'They don't take stroke victims,' Aidan replied coldly.

'I didn't know that... But what else could I have done?' Lindsay looked up at him, shielding her eyes against the sun.

'Did it not occur to you to call me at any time during all this?'

'Yes, it did, as it happens, but I then decided that you would expect me to use my initiative. I was on call, it was up to me to deal with any eventuality. I actually thought I'd coped with the whole thing rather well. That's why I came in here—to tell you. If I'd known how you were going to react I wouldn't have bothered!' With her eyes flashing, she, too, stood up and faced him across the small courtyard.

Afterwards, if anyone had asked her what had happened next she would have been hard put to say. One moment they were facing each other like two protagonists about to enter into combat and the next he'd covered the short distance between them and she was in his arms and his mouth had come down hard onto hers, stifling any further protest she might have been able to make.

The shock was so great that at first she did nothing, then, recovering slightly, she began to struggle. This, however, simply caused him to tighten his hold on her, leaving her helpless against that taut, powerful body.

And it was then that she felt a red-hot shaft of desire somewhere deep inside her. Andrew had never kissed her like this. No one had ever kissed her like this before. Eventually she quite forgot to struggle as he totally overpowered her, until in the end she was responding to him with a fervour she hadn't known she possessed, winding her arms around his neck, sinking her fingers into the short, crisp hair, her kisses every bit as passionate as his.

There had been no one since Andrew. He had been subtle, sophisticated and, she'd thought, what she'd wanted. But this man was raw passion and Lindsay responded to him in a way she'd never responded before as beneath his hands and his mouth one by one her senses came alive.

In the end it was Aidan who pulled away, holding her from him at arm's length. 'My God!' he muttered. 'That shouldn't have happened. I'm sorry,' he said abruptly.

'Don't be,' she whispered.

'But I shouldn't have let it happen.' He spoke as if he was appalled at himself. 'I'm your trainer, for God's sake!'

'I was as much to blame.'

'It makes no difference.' He shook his head, dropping his hands from her shoulders. 'I'm supposed to be in a position of trust. Henry would flay me alive if he knew.'

'Well, he's not going to know, is he?'

He shook his head but it was more a gesture of despair than anything else. Lindsay looked down and saw that both dogs had come up from the garden and were sitting expectantly at their feet. Jess had her head enquiringly on one side as she gazed up at Aidan.

'They're wondering what's happened,' Lindsay said with a shaky smile. 'One moment we were shouting at each other and the next...' She looked up and her gaze met his. He looked away as if he was so embarrassed by what had just happened that he couldn't even look her in the eye.

'Aidan...' Stepping forward, she put her hand on the bare skin of his arm. He reacted sharply, pulling away. 'You'd better go, Lindsay... There may be another call for you.'

Because she carried a mobile phone they were both well aware of the fact that if she was needed she could be reached anywhere, just as they were both well aware that the reason he wanted her to go wasn't because she might be called but because of what had just happened between them.

Her mind was still in turmoil, but where he was covered in confusion and embarrassment she knew she would have been quite happy for him to repeat the whole episode. That, however, seemed most unlikely if the expression on his face was anything to go by, so Lindsay decided her best course of action was to beat a hasty retreat. Pausing only to pat the dogs, she made her way to the steps.

'I'll see you tomorrow,' she said briefly, 'unless, of course, anything else crops up that I think you should know about.'

He followed her to the steps, and as she began to climb he said, 'About Milly...'

'Yes?' She paused again and looked down at him. He was standing with one foot on the bottom step, one hand at the back of his neck—his attitude still one of acute embarrassment. 'What about Milly?'

'I'm sorry I reacted the way I did. You were quite right. There was nothing else you could have done.'

She hesitated. 'Would you have done the same?' she asked curiously.

'Probably,' Aidan admitted. 'I may have tried for somewhere else for Douglas...but you weren't to know.'

She left then, climbing into the Jeep and starting the engine. As she drew away she glanced in her rear-view mirror but he hadn't followed her up the steps to the road.

It was only then that Lindsay realised she was still trembling. If anyone had told her what was going to happen when she went to Aidan's cottage she would never have believed them. Never in a million years would she have believed them. But what had got to her even more than the shock of it happening had been her reaction to it. Her face flamed as she thought of it. Whatever had he thought of her? She must have come across as some sort of hungry man-eater.

How would she be able to face him in the surgery

the next day? She should be ashamed of herself, she told herself sternly as she drove into the village.

She should be, yes, but the truth was, she wasn't ashamed of herself or her actions. Her response to Aidan had been completely spontaneous, as natural as breathing, and she knew, given the chance, she would do exactly the same again.

But Aidan! Aidan of all people. Why, she hadn't even liked him at first. She'd thought him rude, arrogant and self-opinionated, and she was certain he hadn't liked her. He'd criticised everything about her—her clothes, her hair, her background, even her car. They'd argued about so many things. It was true that all that had changed a little in the time she'd been in Tregadfan, and after they'd called their truce things had got better between them, but certainly not to the point where she would have dreamed that he would wish for anything more.

And maybe he didn't want anything more now either. Perhaps he was already regretting his actions. After all, he'd made it perfectly plain that he felt he'd abused Henry's trust in some way. And maybe that would be true if she were some vulnerable young girl who'd been placed in his care. But she wasn't, for heaven's sake! She was a grown woman, with thoughts and feelings of her own.

Lindsay had no idea what would happen next, she only knew that as that fateful weekend drew to a close she found herself awaiting the following day not only with trepidation but also with a delicious sense of anticipation.

'So tell me, what would you be doing this evening if you were in London?' Gwynneth sighed and, with her elbows on the reception desk and her face in her hands, gazed dreamily up at Lindsay.

'You mean if I wasn't working?' said Lindsay drily.

'Oh, yes, of course.' Gwynneth giggled.

'Well...' Lindsay considered. 'If I wasn't working, I would probably take the opportunity of catching up on some sleep.'

'No, I mean if you weren't doing that. If you were going out, where would you go to?' Gwynneth persisted.

'Hmm, let me see. Well, probably I would meet some friends in a wine bar—'

'A wine bar,' breathed Gwynneth. 'I've never been to a wine bar.' She made it sound like some exotic temple and Lindsay couldn't help but smile as she recalled the overcrowded establishments where she and her friends would meet, only to fight for a place at the bar, waiting to be served, followed by the near impossibility of finding a table. 'Afterwards we would perhaps go for a meal—usually Italian or Indian. Sometimes,' she went on, 'we would go to the theatre, or maybe the ballet, or the opera. And occasionally we might go on to a nightclub. But, having said that, I doubt if any of that would have happened on a Monday night.'

'You make it all sound so exciting and so glamorous,' sighed Gwynneth, 'doesn't she, Bronwen? Don't you think it sounds exciting?'

'It's all right if you like that sort of thing,' Bronwen replied waspishly. 'I prefer the quiet life myself. While you, young woman...' She glared at Gwynneth over the half-glasses she wore for close work. 'A few nights of that would finish you. You don't have either the stamina or the constitution for it. One evening of line-dancing in the community hall is about your limit.'

Deflated, Gwynneth fell silent and began filing the last of the morning's medical records, and Lindsay turned to go back to her room. As she did so the door of Aidan's consulting room opened and her heart skipped a beat as he came out into Reception. She'd seen him on a couple of occasions that morning—when he'd first arrived and again in Reception when they'd both been searching for records. Each time she had been intensely aware of him but with the exception of once in Reception when she'd briefly caught his eye and he'd looked quickly away, he'd given no indication that anything untoward had happened between them.

Now she was just as aware of him as he followed her into the staffroom for morning coffee. Henry and Judith were already there. Henry looked up as they came into the room.

'So, how did your first Sunday on call go?' asked Henry as Lindsay poured coffee for herself.

'Fine,' she replied brightly, too brightly probably, aware as she was of Aidan's uncompromising back as he stood at the machine and poured his own coffee.

'No difficult ones?'

'Well, there was one, but I think I coped all right.'

'Was that Mrs Morgan?' asked Judith, looking up from the magazine she was reading and joining in the conversation.

'Yes, it was.' Lindsay nodded.

'I heard about that from Bronwen,' said Henry. Turning to Lindsay, he said, 'Who called you out, Lindsay?'

'Actually, no one did. It was the most incredible co-incidence.' She threw a glance at Aidan but he still had his back to her, then she flicked her tongue over her lips which suddenly felt very dry. 'I was on my way back from another call,' she went on, 'and I decided to call at the Morgans' quite by chance—I'd been there before with Aidan and I knew he liked to keep an eye on them.'

'And you mean you found that Milly had had a stroke?' Judith stared at her in amazement.

'Yes, it had happened some while before but she was on the floor and poor old Douglas, of course, couldn't call anyone.'

'Well, what a bit of luck that you went when you did!' Judith exclaimed.

'Has anyone heard how she is today?' asked Henry, and they all looked at Aidan.

With that he had little option but to turn and face them. 'Yes,' he replied. 'I spoke to the Sister on the medical ward and Milly is as well as can be expected. The next couple of days will, of course, be critical.'

'And Douglas?' asked Lindsay softly. It was then that his gaze, very briefly, met hers.

'I've arranged for Douglas to go to a small nursing home near Rhyl. If Milly recovers sufficiently the staff have agreed to take her as well.'

'Oh, well done,' said Henry. 'They could have been separated, with Douglas spending the rest of his days at Rhondda House and Milly somewhere else. Turning to Lindsay, he said, 'Lindsay, m'dear, do you think you could cope with my late afternoon surgery? I have a meeting later on today—I know it'll go on and on and I shall need to get back to Megan afterwards.'

'Yes, of course.' Lindsay nodded. 'That is, if it's all right with Aidan?'

'Did you have any plans for this young lady this

afternoon, Aidan?' Henry turned to Aidan who hastily shook his head. It was only Lindsay who'd witnessed his slight discomfort at the idea that he might have other plans for her, and she was forced to suppress a smile.

Henry's afternoon surgery was busy, so busy that Lindsay had little time to think about anything else. Not only was she having to cope with someone else's patients, she was also having to cope with patients who'd thought they were going to be seeing Dr Llewellyn. Some seemed rather taken aback then decided it really didn't matter who they saw. One or two were feeling so ill they didn't care just as long as whoever it was they saw gave them some relief from their pain or discomfort. One woman flatly refused to discuss her problems with Lindsay and stomped out of the surgery, saying she would wait until she could see Dr Llewellyn. However, apart from her, they simply kept coming.

And then, at last, just when Lindsay thought it was going on for ever, Gwynneth phoned through to say there was only one more patient to be seen.

'Thank you, Gwynneth,' Lindsay sighed. 'Who is it? I don't seem to have any more records.'

'It's an extra. She's not on the list. Her name is Hannah Sykes.'

'Is that the Baptist minister's daughter?'

'Yes,' Gwynneth replied. 'I'll bring her records down.'

Lindsay barely had time to ease the tension in her aching neck and shoulder muscles before Gwynneth tapped on her door and turned the handle.

'Thanks, Gwynneth.' Lindsay took the record envelope from her then, as the receptionist would have left, she said, 'Has Dr Lennox finished his surgery yet?' She hadn't seen him that afternoon and feared he would be gone before she'd finished. She felt that somehow she couldn't leave things the way they were, that something else needed to be said about what had happened the day before.

'No,' Gwynneth replied. 'He's got three more waiting and he's just been called out on an emergency to Janet Pearce's mother.'

'I see. Well, send Hannah down to me.'

Hannah Sykes was fifteen years old but with her studious expression, wire-framed spectacles and long hair she looked older.

'Come in and sit down, Hannah,' said Lindsay. 'I'm Dr Henderson—I'm sitting in for Dr Llewellyn today.'

'I thought I would be seeing him,' said Hannah.

'Would you rather come back when he's here?' asked Lindsay. By now she was too weary to argue with anyone who would rather not be there.

'Oh, no,' said Hannah swiftly. 'I'd rather see you. Dr Llewellyn's OK, but he knows me very well, and he's a friend of my father's. I don't think I could talk to him. You see, I think I might be pregnant.'

# CHAPTER ELEVEN

'PUT those in Dr Llewellyn's in-tray, please, Bronwen.' Lindsay leaned across the desk and handed her Hannah Sykes's records. 'Oh, and, Bronwen, is Dr Lennox back yet?'

Bronwen shook her head. 'No, and there are still three people waiting to see him.'

'In that case, I'll start seeing them. Send the first one down to my room, please.'

She was exhausted, particularly after her last patient, and she would have liked nothing better than to crawl upstairs to her flat, but the least she could do was to help Aidan out when he was on an emergency.

She saw two of the three patients, one of whom was suffering from an acute case of cystitis and the other was experiencing reflux oesophagitis and was in desperate need of an antacid. On following this last patient out to Reception, Lindsay learnt from Bronwen that Aidan was back and was in his room, seeing the last patient. 'In that case, Bronwen, you and Gwynneth may as well go,' she said. 'I'll drop the catch on the door before I go upstairs then Dr Aidan can see his patient out.'

For once Bronwen didn't argue, and after the two women had gone Lindsay trailed thankfully up the stairs to her flat. Earlier it had been her intention to speak to Aidan but that had been four patients and one emergency down the line and she doubted whether ei-

ther of them would now be up to the sort of personal
discussion she'd had in mind.

It was bliss to kick off her shoes, pour a glass of
wine, switch on her CD player and sink down onto the
sofa and relax. The day had been hectic enough as it
was, but with the added stress of this new awareness
between herself and Aidan, which he seemed to be at
such pains to ignore, there had been moments when
she'd thought she might have been about to explode.

Lindsay had just leaned her head against the back of
the sofa and closed her eyes when there came a knock
at her sitting-room door. Her eyes snapped open again
as her heart skipped a beat. There was only one person
it could be. Only one person who was still in the building. Anyone else would have had to ring through on
the intercom outside the building.

Jumping to her feet, she crossed the room and tugged
open the door. Aidan stood there with one arm leaning
against the doorframe. He, too, looked exhausted.

'You've come to tell me you've finished and you'd
like me to lock up after you, is that it?' she asked,
trying to read the expression in those blue eyes.

He shook his head. 'No,' he said. 'Actually, I've
come to thank you for seeing those two patients of
mine.'

'That's all right.' She shrugged. 'It was the least I
could do.' She paused, half expecting him to go now
that he'd said what he'd come for. But he didn't. He
stayed, looking, she thought, a little sheepish.

'The other thing,' he said, 'is that Gwynneth said
that you wanted to see me.'

'Er, yes, I did. But that was earlier. It's late now and
you must be tired.'

'It's OK. I don't mind. In fact, I wouldn't say no to a glass of that wine you're drinking.'

She looked down surprised to find that the glass was still in her hand. 'You'd better come in,' she said, aware as she did so that her pulse had started to race.

He followed her into the room, pausing as he did so and looking around. 'This looks different from when I was here,' he said. 'A woman's touch was quite obviously what it needed.'

Her hand was shaking as she poured his wine and the neck of the bottle chinked against the edge of the glass. 'I gather you had an emergency,' she said as she handed him the glass. Suddenly she wanted to delay the moment where they talked about themselves.

Aidan nodded, and at her indication sat down in the room's only armchair while Lindsay, in an effort to overcome her nervousness, curled up once more in one corner of the sofa, tucking her legs beneath her.

'It was Audrey Pearce,' he said after a moment, 'Janet's mother. She had a heart attack. Janet called for me but Audrey was in a bad way by the time I got there. I called for an ambulance and I went to the hospital with them. She suffered another massive heart attack on the way and she died before we even reached the hospital.'

'Oh, no.' Lindsay shook her head. 'Poor Janet. How did she take it?'

'She seemed numb. I don't think it had hit her. She's cared for her mother for a very long time.' He paused and took a sip of his wine. 'Anyway, thanks for holding the fort.'

'I've left the two patient's notes I saw in your in-tray.'

'Thanks. Quite straightforward, were they?'

'Yes.' She nodded. 'Not like the last one of Henry's I saw today. That one won't be quite straightforward, I can guarantee. I've left those notes in *his* in-tray.'

'Oh?' Aidan looked up quickly. 'Anything that needs any sort of follow-up tonight?'

'No, nothing like that. It was Hannah Sykes.'

'Peter Sykes's daughter?'

'Yes. She's pregnant.'

'Oh, Lord.' Aidan looked quite stricken. 'How old is she now?'

'Fifteen.'

'Peter and Beth aren't going to be too pleased.'

'No. Quite,' Lindsay agreed.

'Do they know yet?'

'Apparently not. Neither does the father—a boy at her school. Sounds like it was a one-off.'

'I can believe that. I wouldn't have put Hannah down as promiscuous, not given her background and upbringing.'

'They're often the worst. Can't wait to break free, that sort of thing.'

'True,' Aidan admitted. 'But I don't think Peter and Beth have been too restrictive with Hannah or with her brother Paul. This will hit them very hard, especially Peter, in his position.'

'Are they friends of yours?'

'Sort of, though I'd say they were more friends of Henry and Megan. Did Hannah give any indication of what she wanted to do?'

'Not really. I don't think she'd even thought ahead.'

'So what did you do?'

'Well, I confirmed the pregnancy. She's about four months. I also told her that I would tell Henry for her. She's going to try and tell her mother, but I've told her that if she can't then I'll do it for her, or at least be with her when she does so.' Lindsay hesitated. 'Did I do right? I've not been in this situation before.'

'Absolutely,' Aidan replied. 'There wasn't anything else you could have done.'

'I thought I'd leave all the booking forms until we've seen her mother.'

'That's a good idea. I would imagine Hannah has enough to be thinking about for the present.' He was silent for a moment then he allowed his gaze to meet hers. 'Lindsay...I know you wanted to see me, and I also wanted to talk to you. I have the feeling it might be about the same thing.'

'Possibly,' she agreed.

'Well, you go first.'

She took a deep breath. 'All I was going to say was that I can't stand the way it's been between us today. I feel as if I'm walking on eggshells.'

'Me, too.' He nodded. 'I can imagine how you must be feeling after my appalling behaviour, and what I wanted to say was that I'll quite understand if you don't wish to remain here. I'll even go so far as to say that I'm quite prepared to explain the situation to Henry.'

'Aidan...please...' With a spontaneous gesture Lindsay scrambled to her feet.

'No.' He, too, stood up. 'Hear me out—please. I know sexual harassment in a working situation constitutes a grave offence and I can only apologise once again—'

'Sexual harassment? Oh, Aidan, stop, please.' She stared at him, not knowing whether to laugh or be serious, then, seeing his misery, she lifted her hand and gently touched the tiny scar on his cheek. Helplessness melted the ice blue of his eyes. 'How can it have been sexual harassment when I responded in the way I did?' she said softly.

He shook his head. 'I don't know. All I know is I feel wretched about it and about what you must think of me.'

'And don't you think there's a chance I might be feeling bad about what you must be thinking about me?'

'What do you mean?' He frowned and lifted his own hand to take hold of hers, moving it away from his cheek but not releasing it.

'Well, I thought you must be thinking that I must be some sort of man-eater, the way I reacted, and since then...well, you've practically ignored me and I didn't know what to think.'

'Are you trying to say that I'm forgiven?' His voice was husky now.

'There's nothing to forgive, Aidan, really there isn't. But...' she paused '...there is one thing I should like to know.'

'What's that?' Still he held onto her hand. His grip was firm and warm and Lindsay felt as if something deep inside her had started to melt.

'Why did you do it?'

He stared at her. 'Well...I...' he floundered.

'Was it a spur-of-the-moment impulse? Because one moment you were bawling me out, and the next... well!'

'Bawling you out, as you put it, was one of the methods I'd adopted for keeping myself in check,' he said huskily. As he spoke Lindsay was aware that he'd allowed his gaze to roam from her eyes to her hair then finally to her mouth, where it lingered. 'Don't you realise how hard it has been for me, Lindsay? Don't you have any idea of the way I feel about you?'

Deep inside her the melting sensation had given way to a deep throb of desire. 'Tell me,' she whispered.

'I'm not sure you would want to hear this,' he replied.

'Try me.'

'I've wanted you from the moment I set eyes on you.' He spoke quietly but precisely, his eyes not leaving her mouth for one moment. 'At first I tried to deny it by telling myself that you quite simply weren't my type, that we were like chalk and cheese. You were a city girl. I was the proverbial country boy. You were sleek and sophisticated, everything I wasn't. I knew you wouldn't look twice at me so I put up the barricades from the word go.'

'How do you know I wouldn't have looked twice at you?' she demanded softly.

'You'd made it perfectly plain you weren't happy to have me as your trainer. I took that to mean you wouldn't have been too happy having me play any other role in your life either, so again I thought it best to keep my distance. It was even harder after we'd called our truce and agreed to start again. We quite naturally became friends and I found it even more difficult to keep you at arm's length. The day you came to Capel Curig with me was like some sort of exquisite torture…'

'So what happened yesterday?' Lindsay sounded mystified. 'What had changed?'

'It was you,' Aidan admitted. 'My adrenalin was already flowing from splitting those logs and I looked up and there you were. Honestly, I thought I was hallucinating for a moment. You stood there so cool and fresh in that blue skirt and there was me sweating and, well, I wanted you so much, and then you started telling me about Milly. I even pretended I was angry with you just to help me keep my distance and then…then when *you* got angry…well, that did it. I just lost it…'

'Oh, Aidan…come here.' Taking her hand from his, she took his face in both her hands and gazed into his eyes.

'Don't play with me, Lindsay.' His voice was low now with a dangerous edge to it. 'Because, I warn you, if you do you could be playing with fire. I know there's no way you could ever feel the same way about me and accept that. But I do have feelings and there's only a certain amount I can take.'

'Why do you assume I couldn't feel the same way about you?'

'You just couldn't, that's all. It's like I said. We're poles apart—you a town girl with all your talk of London, your parties, your wine bars and trips to the theatre, your holidays in the sun, and me with my dogs, my cottage and the wild Welsh countryside…'

'What if I were to tell you that I also felt something between us almost from the start? That I also denied it, partly because I was still feeling raw from my last relationship and partly because you were being so objectionable that I had to keep telling myself that I couldn't possibly even like you, let alone anything else. But then yesterday, when that happened and you started to kiss me, all I knew was that I didn't want you to stop.'

'Do you really mean that?' Aidan looked astounded.

'Of course I do.' Still holding his face between her hands, Lindsay raised herself onto her toes then kissed him gently on his lips. 'So do you think, Dr Lennox,' she murmured between kisses, 'that you could carry on where you left off, please, because I don't think I can wait much longer?'

They agreed to try and keep it a secret, just between themselves, at least for a little longer, but it proved to be a bitter-sweet secret for there was a part of Lindsay that longed to shout of her love from the rooftops. Instead, she had to make do with longing glances when they thought no one else was looking, the secret touching of hands or a stolen kiss when they had a rare moment alone.

'I know I shall have to tell Henry,' said Aidan one morning later in the week when they'd returned from a couple of house calls and were sitting together in his Land Rover outside the surgery, delaying the moment when they would have to go inside. 'I'm just putting it off.'

'Do you really think his reaction will be that bad?' asked Lindsay anxiously.

'I think once he gets used to the idea he'll probably be delighted for the pair of us...'

'Well, then, why not just go for it and get it over with?'

'Because I'm not sure where we stand ethically. I've never heard of a trainer and a trainee having a relationship before. Henry may consider it necessary to terminate the arrangement and send you straight back to London. I'm not sure I could cope with that.'

'I can't see the problem. Husband-and-wife GPs work together all the time.'

'That's different,' said Aidan darkly.

'Come on,' said Lindsay. 'We'd best go in. If

Bronwen cranes her neck much further to try and see what we're up to, she'll fall out of that window.'

Aidan chuckled and, climbing out of the Land Rover, followed Lindsay into the building. 'Maybe,' he murmured as he caught her up in the doorway, 'I should have given you a kiss in full view of staff and patients alike. That would really give them something to talk about.'

Lindsay was still smiling after they'd entered the building and passed Bronwen's suspicious stare and Gwynneth's bright-eyed, eager look before she and Aidan diverged to their separate consulting rooms.

If she was honest she was still reeling from what was happening between herself and Aidan. It had been surprising to the point of being shocking, and yet there was an inevitability about it that simply demanded acceptance, as if the whole thing was beyond their control and being orchestrated by some force greater than either of them. But whatever it was, it had the effect of rendering her almost helpless, to the point where she could hardly bear to be away from him.

She had barely time to remove her jacket and sit down behind her desk when her intercom buzzed. She flicked the switch, expecting it to be Gwynneth or Bronwen, but surprisingly it was Henry's voice she heard.

'Lindsay,' he said. 'I thought I saw you come in. Could you spare me a few moments, please, before you start surgery?'

'Of course, Henry. Shall I come along to your room?'

'Yes, please.'

It wasn't until she was halfway along the passage that it dawned on her that Henry had sounded a little strange. Usually if he wanted to say something to her he popped into her room. This sounded serious or at least important. Was it Megan? Had something happened? She quickened her pace and had actually reached Reception before the possibility dawned on her that maybe Henry knew about Aidan and herself. Had he seen something? Or heard something? They had been so careful. But in a village like Tregadfan didn't everyone know everything about everyone else? Was it impossible to have any secret?

Her heart was thumping uncomfortably by the time she'd knocked on Henry's door and he'd bidden her enter. He was standing with his back to the door, gazing out of the window. It was a relief to find him alone. For one awful moment Lindsay had expected to find Aidan there as well. On second thoughts, maybe that wouldn't have been a bad thing—that way they could have faced the music together. There was no more time to speculate, however, for Henry turned from the window.

'Ah, Lindsay,' he said, 'come in, please, and sit down.'

Closing the door carefully behind her, Lindsay crossed the room and sat down facing him while Henry took the chair behind the desk.

'Lindsay, a situation has arisen which I am forced to address.' Henry made a steeple with his hands, pressing his two index fingers against his mouth as he carefully considered his words.

Here it comes, thought Lindsay wildly. He's going to say it has come to his attention that his partner and his trainee are in the midst of a torrid affair. Well, if that's the case, I shall say it simply isn't true. You can hardly call it an affair when we haven't even been to bed. I shall say...I shall...

Suddenly she realised that Henry was speaking again and had mentioned Megan's name, but she'd been so embroiled in her own thoughts that she hadn't heard any more. Megan. Lindsay's head jerked up. So was that what this was all about? Had she been right on her first guess after all? 'Is Megan all right?' she blurted out.

Henry paused and looked at her over his hands. 'Megan?' he said.

'Yes, you said something about Megan.'

'Only that she'd had a visit from her friend, Juliet, who helps her run her craft shop in the village.'

'Oh, so Megan's all right, then?' Lindsay frowned, out of her depth now.

'Well, she's no worse...'

'Thank goodness. I thought for one moment you were going to tell me that something had happened to Megan.'

'No, nothing like that. I'm sorry, Lindsay, if I startled you.' Henry stared at her in concern. 'You've gone quite pale.'

'It's OK,' Lindsay mumbled. 'So, what were you saying about this Juliet?'

'She went to see Megan yesterday afternoon and she told her something that I find rather disconcerting.'

'Oh?' Lindsay frowned, wondering again what on earth she was about to hear and whether her sense of relief over hearing that Megan was no worse was about to be shattered as her relationship with Aidan was exposed after all.

'Yes,' mused Henry. 'She told Megan that she'd heard in the village that Hannah Sykes was pregnant.'

'What?' Lindsay stared at him. 'But no one knows that yet.'

'That's what I thought,' Henry replied. 'You said she'd made an appointment to come here with her mother to see you?'

Lindsay nodded. 'They're coming in this afternoon.'

'So who else knows about Hannah, apart from you and I?''

'Only Aidan. I told him at the time to make sure I was handling it properly.'

'And Hannah hadn't told anyone else?'

'She said no. Not even the boy responsible knows.'

'I suppose there's always a chance she told a friend. What does concern me is that the leak came from here.'

'But how could it when only the three of us knew?'

Henry was silent for a moment, drumming his fingers on the desk. Then, looking up, slowly he said, 'Presumably the staff could have known?'

'Well, yes, I suppose so. I put it on the computer and in Hannah's notes and, of course, I did a urine test. But...' Lindsay bit her lip '...even if they did, surely no one would say anything. It would be a direct breach of confidence and I can't imagine that either Bronwen or Gwynneth would do that. I doubt whether even Judith could have known, and then there's only Mrs Jones, and she would only have known if she'd heard any of the others talking about it.'

'You have to admit, it amounts to a pretty irresistible bit of gossip—the Baptist minister's fifteen-year-old daughter pregnant.'

'What will you do?'

'Nothing for the moment.' Henry stood up. 'I want to speak to Megan again first. At least by this afternoon the girl's mother will know.' He sighed. 'That is, if she hasn't already heard it elsewhere.'

Lindsay returned to her consulting room with a heavy heart. She hoped desperately that Henry didn't think that she'd been guilty of betraying a patient's confidentiality. The poor man had enough to worry about as it was without this. A swift stab of guilt hit her when she remembered that he knew nothing yet about herself and Aidan. Would that also simply add to his burden?

During the course of the morning she decided that she would talk to Aidan and put it to him that they tell Henry what was happening between them.

When, however, they all met up in the staffroom at the end of the morning, all such resolutions fled from her mind when she caught sight of the expression on Henry's face. He'd apparently already told Aidan about the leak concerning Hannah Sykes. Now, as he joined them and Lindsay poured him a coffee, it was Aidan who broached the dreaded question.

'Any further development, Henry?' he asked.

Henry nodded grimly. 'Yes,' he replied, 'and of the worse possible kind.' When the other two remained silent, he said, 'I rang Megan and asked her if she would ask her friend Juliet where she'd heard about Hannah Sykes. Juliet told her that she'd overheard a conversation in the local library between two women. Because there appeared to be nothing secret about the conversation, Juliet had imagined that the content was common knowledge.

'Did she know who the women were?' asked Aidan.

'Oh, yes,' Henry replied. 'One was the butcher's wife and the other, the one who imparted the information, was…Bronwen Matthews.'

Lindsay drew in her breath sharply.

'I shall deal with the matter straight away,' Henry went on. 'I just wanted the pair of you to know before I do so.'

'You'll dismiss her, of course,' said Aidan.

'Absolutely,' Henry replied. 'It's clearly stated in the staff contract that any breach of confidentiality will result in instant dismissal.'

'How will Gwynneth manage on her own?' asked Lindsay.

'We'll just have to help her as much as we can until we can appoint someone else.' With that Henry left the staffroom to carry out the onerous task that, as senior partner, now fell to him.

'Poor old Henry,' said Aidan as the door shut behind the older man. 'He hates this sort of thing, but it just shows you never can tell. I would have staked my life on Bronwen's loyalty to the practice.'

'I was thinking that we should come clean and confess to Henry about us,' said Lindsay after a moment. 'I'd hate him to find that out from someone else as well.'

'I agree,' Aidan replied. 'But maybe right now isn't exactly a good time. There will be anger and stamping around from Bronwen and, I imagine, floods of tears from Gwynneth.'

'But Bronwen terrorised Gwynneth,' protested Lindsay. 'I would have thought she'd be glad to see the back of her.'

'I shouldn't count on it,' said Aidan darkly. 'There's no telling with Gwynneth—she'll probably feel sorry for Bronwen now.'

# CHAPTER TWELVE

'SO GELERT was a dog?' Lindsay rolled over in the long grass so that she could look down the hill to the village of Beddgelert below them.

Aidan nodded and eased himself alongside her. 'Yes.' He pointed. 'His grave is down there.'

'So what is the legend?' asked Lindsay.

'Many years ago,' said Aidan, 'according to Welsh folklore, Gelert's master, a prince, had left him guarding his baby son. When the prince returned the hound came to meet him with blood around his mouth. There was no sign of the baby and the prince thought Gelert had attacked and killed him so he, in turn, drew his sword and put the dog to death.'

'And had he killed the baby?'

'No. The baby had been dragged away and was found safe and sound beside the body of a wolf. The prince then realised that Gelert had saved the baby by killing the wolf and it was the wolf's blood he had seen and not the baby's. He felt so remorseful that he had the faithful dog buried with great ceremony and his grave is marked to this day.'

'What a sad story,' said Lindsay. Turning to look at Jess and Skipper, who were stretched out in the sun beside them, she said, 'It just goes to prove the loyalty and devotion of a dog, doesn't it?'

'Absolutely. It's a pity some humans didn't show the same loyalty.'

'You're thinking of Bronwen,' she said.

Aidan sighed and rolled onto his back. 'I would never have thought it of her,' he said. 'I suppose it just goes to show you never can tell.'

'What do you think she'll do?'

'Goodness knows. It won't be easy to get another job. Not in Tregadfan. It wouldn't surprise me if she didn't move away.'

'But where would she go?'

'She has family near Llangollen—it's my guess she'll go to them.'

They were silent for a moment, reflecting on what had happened the previous week at the surgery. It was quiet and peaceful up here in their vantage point above Beddgelert, the only sound being the hum of a light aircraft overhead, the bleating of sheep and the distant peal of church bells.

It was Lindsay who broke the silence because suddenly she had to know. Taking a piece of grass, she began tracing it gently over Aidan's face. 'Talking of Bronwen,' she said, 'was there ever anything between the two of you?' She'd half expected him to give a shout of incredulous laughter, but he didn't.

'Why do you ask?' he said, opening one eye and staring up at her.

'I had the feeling once or twice that Bronwen regarded you as her exclusive property. She also seemed to resent me and the fact that you were my trainer—I just wondered, that's all.'

'There wasn't anything between Bronwen and myself,' said Aidan at last. 'But that's not to say she wouldn't have liked there to have been. She made that plain on more than one occasion.'

'And you?' she said softly, stopping her tracing.

'No,' he replied firmly. 'Never in a million years.

And I'd made that quite plain almost from the moment I joined the practice.'

'So it wasn't Bronwen who betrayed you?'

'Betrayed me?' He frowned, squinting at her against the glare of the sun.

'Yes, when I told you about Andrew and the way he'd betrayed me, I got the impression that you, too, had been betrayed because you seemed to know exactly how I felt.'

'Yes,' Aidan agreed. 'I did know because it had happened to me. But it had nothing to do with Bronwen.' He paused and for one moment Lindsay thought that even now he wasn't going to enlighten her further, then he sighed. 'It was a long time ago. After my father died my mother and I carried on living in our home in Ireland until I came to England to study medicine. There was a girl in Ireland. Her name was Sineard. I loved her and I thought she loved me and would wait for me.'

'But she didn't?' asked Lindsay softly.

'No. She ended up marrying the boy who had been my best friend at school.'

'So yours was a double betrayal?'

'Yes, I suppose you could say that.'

'So you really did know how I felt?' she whispered, leaning across him as she did so.

'Oh, yes, I knew. Only too well,' he replied. Reaching out his hand, he caught her arm, the one supporting her weight, so that she fell across him. The next moment he'd rolled over so that he was on top of her then he lowered his head, blotting out the sun as his mouth covered hers.

She'd been prepared to ask him more about this woman, about his life in Ireland, about his mother even, but as he parted her lips with his tongue that fierce desire was ignited once more and within moments she was clinging helplessly to him. As his hands moved, moulding her breasts and hips through the thin fabric of her dress, her body throbbed and ached and clamoured for more.

It was the insistent ringing of the mobile phone that interrupted them only seconds from the point of no return.

At first Lindsay thought he was going to ignore it, but in the end years of discipline and medical training took over.

'Damn!' Aidan groaned as he reached over to where his jacket lay on the grass and retrieved his phone from the pocket.

'Henry,' she heard him say after he'd answered the persistent ringing. A silence followed as he listened, then he said, 'We're at Beddgelert. Yes, we could come back that way.' Another silence. 'Yes, Lindsay is here with me.'

Pulling a face, he switched off the phone. 'Come on, Dr Henderson,' he said scrambling to his feet and offering his hand to help her up. 'We are on a mercy mission.'

'What is it?' she asked. The dogs, startled by the sudden activity, rose to their feet and began stretching themselves and yawning.

'Clarrie Williams has gone into labour,' Aidan replied. 'The district midwife's car has broken down out on the Glasfryn road—she's waiting for the rescue service—and Henry has a call to go to Gwytherin. Both of those places are in the opposite direction from the Williamses' place near Capel Curig.'

'So what are we waiting for?' Taking Aidan's hand,

Lindsay led the way down the steep, rocky path to where the Land Rover was parked in a clearing. A mountain stream tumbled beside them, crashing so noisily onto rocks at the bottom that further conversation was impossible until they were inside the vehicle, with the dogs installed in the back.

'Let's hope Clarrie can hold on until we get there,' said Aidan as they pulled out of the clearing onto the narrow mountain road. 'Fourth babies are usually pretty impatient to be born.'

They were silent for a while as Aidan put his foot down and drove as fast as the tortuous roads would permit.

'Was Henry surprised that I was with you?' Lindsay said at last, throwing him a curious glance. 'With it being our day off, I mean.'

'Actually, I don't think he was,' Aidan replied with a grin.

'So what did he say?' Lindsay persisted, 'when you said I was with you?'

'It wasn't so much what he said but the way that he said it.'

'How do you mean?'

'When I said that, yes, you were with me, he simply said, "Ah."'

'Do you think he knows about us?'

'I'm beginning to think he might have a pretty good idea.'

'We have to say something soon.'

'Yes, I know. I thought we'd just let all the uproar over Bronwen die down first.'

'It's going to be difficult at the surgery with just Gwynneth there,' said Lindsay after a while. 'Do you think it will be too hard to find someone else?' she added.

'Actually, I think I might know just the person.'

'Really?' Lindsay threw him a surprised look. 'I thought it was practically impossible to get suitable staff.'

'It is, under normal conditions, but sometimes one of life's little coincidences happen. I haven't said anything yet, but I think that Janet Pearce may well be interested in coming to work for us.'

'Janet? But her mother's only just died.'

'I know,' Aidan replied, 'and she will, of course, need time. But once the funeral is over and her mother's affairs are in order, it may well be just what she needs.'

'But didn't you say she was a staff nurse? Won't she want to return to that?'

'Janet once told me that she'd been out of nursing for far too long and was too out of touch to be able to pick up the threads again. But with her medical background I think she would be great in the surgery. What do you think?'

'Well, yes,' Lindsay agreed. 'If it's what she wants, of course.'

'She once told me that if her mother died she would have to find employment until she reaches retirement age. She's only in her mid-fifties.'

'How do you think she and Gwynneth would get on?'

'I think it could be an excellent combination. Janet is a gentle soul and Gwynneth would respond to that, but at the same time Janet has an excellent brain on her with a flair for order and efficiency. I think they would make a good team.'

'At least Gwynneth won't be terrorised any more.'

'You mean, by Bronwen?'

'Yes, she made her life an absolute misery.'

He frowned. 'I didn't know it was that bad. You should have said.'

'Gwynneth begged me not to.' Lindsay sighed. 'I wish I had now. Have you said anything to Henry about this yet?'

Aidan shook his head. 'No, I thought I'd get your reaction first.'

'Well, provided it's what Janet wants, I think it's a wonderful idea.'

Rufus met them in the yard. He looked agitated as if all the cares of the world were on his thin shoulders. Lindsay felt sorry for him.

'Where's your mum?' asked Aidan as he and Lindsay hurried behind the boy into the farmhouse.

'She's upstairs in the bedroom,' Rufus replied briefly. There was no time today for looking at geese or stopping to chat with anyone. Evie was in one corner of the living room a terrified expression in her huge eyes. A boy was with her whom Lindsay presumed was the other son, Jared. Dai was at the top of the stairs.

'Thank God you've come, Doctor,' he called when he caught sight of Aidan. 'Come up—there's something wrong. I'm sure there is. It's all much more difficult than any of the others.'

Lindsay ran up the stairs behind Aidan and followed him into the overcrowded, untidy bedroom. Clarrie was lying on the bed dressed only in a cotton nightdress. Her skin looked a greyish colour and there was a film of sweat over her face and neck. Her hair, lank and straight, was plastered to her head while her hands had

gathered up great bunches of bedclothes. Even before
they were properly in the room a contraction seized her
swollen body and she twisted the material in her hands
as a desperate cry left her lips.

'It's all right, Clarrie, we're here now.' Aidan swept
a space clear on the top of a chest of drawers and set
down his case. 'Let's have a look at you and see what
this baby is up to.' Swiftly he took latex gloves from
his case and pulled them on. Then, after Lindsay had
folded back the bedclothes and lifted Clarrie's nightdress, he proceeded to examine her.

When he'd finished he straightened up, then indicated for Lindsay to join him by the window.

'What is it?' she murmured. 'Is there anything
wrong?'

'She's about seven centimetres dilated but the baby
is in a face-to-pubes position instead of the usual way.'

'Won't that mean a forceps delivery?' asked Lindsay
in the same low tones.

'Not necessarily. Sometimes a baby will turn naturally, or if it doesn't and the mother doesn't get too
tired—one of these can sometimes mean a long labour—she'll be able to deliver normally. I'm sure
that's what Clarrie will want.'

'But is the baby all right?' Lindsay persisted anxiously.

'Foetal heartbeat is fine,' Aidan replied. 'I'm going
to ring Sister Mackett on her mobile and see if she has
any idea what time she'll get here. If Clarrie is going
to deliver naturally she'll be wanting some gas and air,
and I don't have that.'

'What is it?' demanded Dai. He was standing in the
doorway, supporting his weight on his elbow crutches.
'There's something wrong, isn't there?'

'Not really, Dai.' It was Aidan who answered him. 'We have a situation where the baby is in an unusual position.'

'I don't want to go to hospital,' Clarrie had lifted herself up in the bed.

'OK, Clarrie. I'm hoping that won't be necessary,' Aidan replied. 'Baby's heartbeat is nice and strong— it's just whether or not you'll get too tired before the birth.'

'I won't.' Determinedly Clarrie bit down on her lower lip.

'In that case, I think we'll get ourselves a bit organised here,' said Aidan. 'Sister Mackett will have a fit if she arrives and there's nothing ready.'

'I'll sort things out,' said Lindsay, aware as she spoke that Aidan threw her a grateful look. 'Dai, do you think you and the boys could organise tea for everyone? And, Clarrie...' she turned to the bed '...if you tell me where everything is for the baby, I'll set it out.'

'It's all in the cupboard over there.' Clarrie nodded towards a large corner cupboard. 'The cradle is in the other bedroom. I wasn't due till next week. All the others were late. Ah...' She gasped as another contraction shook her.

A call to the midwife revealed that she was still awaiting the arrival of the rescue service. Aidan briefly put her in the picture and told her that all was well because Clarrie had no fewer than two doctors in attendance.

While Aidan kept a close watch on the baby's progress Lindsay proceeded to tidy the bedroom, folding up clothes or hanging them in the wardrobe. She carried the wooden cradle into the room and set it at the foot of the bed, then she opened the cupboard to find its shelves stacked with baby clothes and toiletries. It was quite easily the neatest corner of the house, proving beyond doubt that if everything else had become too much for Clarrie in recent months she was obviously determined to be fully prepared for the birth of her baby.

After a while Rufus brought tea for everyone. On entering the bedroom, he threw a fearful glance at his mother, as if dreading what he might be about to see.

'It's all right, Rufus.' Aidan intercepted the glance. 'Your mum is doing just fine. There's a bet on at the moment to see who arrives first—the baby or Sister Mackett.' He paused then, looking at Clarrie, he said, 'Was Dai present when the others were born, Clarrie?'

She nodded. 'Yes...all of them,' she said.

'In that case, Rufus, tell your dad to come up when he's drunk his tea. We can't have him missing this one.'

By this time Lindsay had made up the cradle and finished her preparations for the birth. Picking up one of the mugs of tea, she took a sip. 'Anything else I can do?' she said, her gaze meeting Aidan's.

'If this baby wins the race and gets here before the midwife, how would you like to deliver it?'

'Well... I... It's a long time since I delivered a baby,' she murmured.

'Then it'll be good experience for you,' Aidan replied firmly. 'We GPs never know when we're going to be called upon. Perhaps you'd like to check and see if there's any progress while we've all been guzzling our tea.'

Apprehensively Lindsay donned a pair of latex gloves. It had indeed been a long time since she'd delivered a baby. It had been back in her training days in London during her stint in obstetrics. Carefully she examined Clarrie.

'The foetal heart is still strong,' she reported to Aidan a few minutes later. As she spoke another huge contraction gripped Clarrie.

'I want to push…' she grunted. The contraction died away and Lindsay checked the cervix.

'Ten centimetres dilated and I can feel the anterior fontanelle.'

'Where's Dai?' gasped Clarrie as another contraction seized her.

'I'm right here, love.' Unbeknown to either Aidan or Lindsay, Dai had come back into the bedroom. Moving to the head of the bed, he sat down and took hold of Clarrie's hand.

'Clarrie's in a hurry now,' said Aidan cheerfully. 'She and the baby have decided not to bother about gas and air, neither are they going to wait for Sister Mackett.'

'I'm going…to…push again…' Clarrie's face went purple with exertion.

'Will everything be all right?' asked Dai anxiously, looking over his shoulder at the two doctors at the foot of the bed. 'What with the baby being in the wrong position and Sister Mackett not being here?'

'Everything's fine, Dai,' said Aidan calmly. 'Dr Henderson here is going to deliver the baby. She's one of the finest baby doctors in the country. It's a privilege to have her here.'

Lindsay looked up sharply and as her startled gaze met Aidan's he winked at her. Then Clarrie's actions demanded her attention once more.

'Baby's head has crowned,' Lindsay announced triumphantly some while later. 'Now, Clarrie, I want you to pant for me... Yes, that's right, like that. I can see you've done this before. Well done.' Vaguely, out of the corner of her eye she was aware that Aidan was drawing up an injection. For the life of her she couldn't think what it could be.

At last the baby's head was born with its face uppermost instead of in the usual position, and it was then that Aidan administered the injection to Clarrie. 'Syn-ometrine,' he murmured to Lindsay, 'to prevent the risk of a haemorrhage in the final stage of labour.'

'Of course,' said Lindsay, remembering. Then, following a further contraction, gently but firmly she guided the baby into the world—first the tiny shoulders, quickly followed by another contraction which expelled the rest of its body.

'It's a girl,' said Lindsay triumphantly, at the same time lifting the baby onto Clarrie's chest. 'She's beautiful, just beautiful.' She gulped as tears suddenly filled her eyes, momentarily obscuring her vision.

While Clarrie and Dai were welcoming their new daughter Lindsay clamped and cut the umbilical cord and a little later delivered the placenta. It was at that moment that Sister Mackett arrived.

'I can see,' she said as she bustled into the bedroom and was greeted by a ring of happy faces, 'that I'm not needed here.'

'Hello, Sister,' said Clarrie. 'I'm afraid the baby couldn't wait for you.'

'What do we have?' Sister Mackett leaned over the bed to look at the tiny, crumpled face.

'A little girl.' There were still tears in Dai's eyes as he answered.

'The children are desperate to come up,' said Sister

Mackett. 'It'll be a bit over crowded in here but I think we should let them, just for a moment.'

'Oh, yes,' said Clarrie. 'They must meet their new sister.'

The older children crowded into the bedroom—Rufus shy and embarrassed, Jared wary and Evie so eager that she almost hurled herself at her mother and had to be restrained by Dai. They all dutifully kissed their mother and examined the baby, and were just on the point of being shooed out by Sister Mackett again when Jared, who'd reached the door, paused and looked back. 'Does she have a name?' he asked.

Clarrie glanced at Dai who gave a tiny nod. 'Yes,' she said with a little sigh of contentment. 'She does now. We couldn't decide before, but now we're both agreed—it has to be Lindsay.'

'Well, I would say that just about clinches it,' said Aidan as later they drew away from the farm.

'What clinches what?' Lindsay had been waving to Dai and the children who had all crowded into the yard to see them off, but she turned now and looked at Aidan beside her.

'Having a baby named after you. I would say your acceptance amongst the locals has been well and truly confirmed.'

Lindsay flushed. 'You think so?'

'I know so.' He nodded. 'That particular family have really taken you to their hearts. Mind you, I can't say I blame them.' Taking one hand from the steering-wheel, he covered hers and squeezed it tightly. 'That was a great job you did. Well done. I was proud of you.'

'I feel quite light-headed.' She gave a little sigh. 'It's an experience to even watch a birth but to actually deliver a baby—well, that's something else. I had a job to keep my emotions under control—I have to confess I very nearly disgraced myself and had a good howl.'

'You may not have been the only one,' he admitted sheepishly.

'You, too?' She raised her eyebrows, surprised to hear him admit to such a thing.

'Every time.' He nodded. 'It really gets to me.'

'I must say they all seemed in a happier frame of mind since the last time we were there.'

'Dai told me he's started his physiotherapy,' said Aidan. 'A neighbour has agreed to take him in twice a week. Maybe at last they can begin to see an end to their troubles.'

'Oh, I do hope so,' Lindsay replied.

They drove on towards Tregadfan and had almost reached the village when Aidan spoke again. 'Lindsay,' he said quietly, and there was something about the tone of his voice that let her know that what he was about to say was serious. She turned her head to look at him but waited in silence for him to continue, at the same time studying his profile—those features which in such a short space of time had become so familiar and so dear to her.

'I think we should go and see Henry,' he said quietly. 'I think we should tell him.'

'I thought you said we should wait until all the fuss over Bronwen had died down.'

'I know I did. But I would hate him to hear it from anyone else, and the way things are between us—well, I don't think I can hide my feelings for much longer. I love you, Lindsay, and I want everyone to know it.'

Pulling the Land Rover to the side of the road, he switched off the engine. Leaning across, he pulled her into his arms and covered her lips with his own in a kiss so full of longing that her pulse began to race.

From the rear of the vehicle Jess gave a single sharp bark but when she realised that no one was about to get out she settled down again, her nose on her paws.

When at last they drew apart Lindsay spoke. 'What will we do,' she said, 'if Henry says you can no longer be my trainer?'

'You mean, if the worst came to the worst and you had to return to London to continue your training? Well, I guess I'd just have to come with you and find another job.'

'You'd do that?' she asked wonderingly, allowing her gaze to roam over his face.

'Absolutely,' he replied unhesitatingly. 'I couldn't bear to be away from you now and there's no way I intend to risk losing you.'

'Oh, Aidan,' she whispered. 'You won't lose me, whatever happens—I promise you that.' Reaching up, she touched his cheek with her fingers. 'And let's face it,' she went on after a moment, 'there's always the chance that Henry knows anyway and will say it doesn't matter and that you can carry on as my trainer even if we are in love.'

'Well,' he replied, 'there's only one way to find out.' Drawing away from her, he turned the key in the ignition.

The shadows were lengthening by the time they reached the Llewellyns' house.

'Looks like they have company,' said Aidan as they drew in alongside an unfamiliar car parked on the drive.

'Maybe now is not the best time...' Lindsay began. 'Perhaps we should go...'

'Too late,' Aidan replied. 'Henry has seen us.' A movement in the window was followed by the opening of the front door.

'Aidan.' Henry stood in the doorway. There was a guarded expression on his face. 'Did everything go all right?'

Aidan nodded. 'Yes, Clarrie had a daughter. Lindsay delivered her.'

'Well done, Lindsay.' Henry turned to her but there was a weariness about him. 'I'm glad you've come,' he added shortly. 'You have a visitor.'

'A visitor?' said Lindsay in surprise as they followed Henry into the house.

'Yes.' Henry nodded. 'He's in here.' Opening the study door, he stood back for Lindsay to precede him into the room.

Briefly she wondered if her visitor was her father, thinking how appropriate that would be, how he could meet Aidan, but as she crossed the threshold she stopped and her heart seemed to turn over as the man standing by the window turned to face her and she saw that it was Andrew Barlow.

# CHAPTER THIRTEEN

'ANDREW!' Lindsay stared at him in astonishment, only vaguely aware that Henry had withdrawn from the room and shut the door behind her. 'What on earth are you doing here?'

He drew in his breath sharply, his nostrils flaring— a gesture she'd once found attractive. 'I've come to take you home, Lindsay.'

'Take me home? Whatever do you mean?' She continued to stare at him. A thought suddenly struck her, and in sudden alarm she said, 'There's nothing wrong, is there? My father...is he all right?'

'As far as I know, yes.' Andrew frowned. 'Lindsay, it's you I've come about. It's high time you stopped all this nonsense and came home.'

'What are you talking about,' she demanded, 'and what do you mean by nonsense?' She faced him across Henry's study, only too aware that Aidan was in the other room and of what they'd come here to discuss. What he must be thinking of Andrew turning up like this out of the blue, she had no idea.

'This whole thing,' said Andrew in answer to her question, throwing wide one hand in a gesture, as if including the whole area. 'This running away to Wales.'

'I haven't run away to Wales,' she retorted. 'I'm here in Wales to do a job. I'm undertaking my GP training—'

'But surely you didn't have to come all this way for

that! Wasn't there somewhere in London you could have done the same thing?'

'Yes, I dare say there was,' she replied, stung by his attitude. 'But I chose not to stay in London—'

'You were running away,' he repeated.

'Running away from what?'

'From the unfortunate situation that had arisen between us.'

'Unfortunate situation...' She stared at him, speechless at his audacity. 'Is that what you called it?' She managed to speak at last but the words threatened to choke her. 'I called it infidelity...'

'Oh, hardly that, Lindsay,' he protested. 'Come on, we weren't married—we weren't even engaged, come to that.'

'We were living together, Andrew,' she said tightly. 'Maybe to you that didn't mean anything, but as far as I was concerned we'd made a commitment. I'm not in the habit of inviting men to share my home.'

'Well, no...' for the briefest of moments he had the grace to look shamefaced then the same old confident smile was firmly back in place, its object as always to charm her into submission. 'Lindsay, come on. I told you how sorry I was at the time. I'll say it again now and then perhaps we can forget the whole thing. We can't just throw away everything we had—we were so good together. Now, you can't deny that, can you?' He moved towards her as if he was about to take her in his arms. Hastily she sidestepped.

'No, Andrew,' she replied, moving towards the window. 'I can't deny it—it was good between us for a time. But that was then. There *is* no us now.'

'But there could be,' he argued. 'If it was good once, it could be again!'

'No, Andrew. It couldn't because I don't trust you any more.'

'But you would, Lindsay—'

'No, I wouldn't. I would always be wondering where you were, who you were with and whether or not you'd do it again. I'm sorry, Andrew, but it really is over.'

'But I thought you loved me.'

'So did I.'

He stared at her in apparent exasperation. 'I still say this whole thing is ridiculous,' he said at last. 'If you were only to stop all this nonsense and come right back to London with me now then we could start again.'

For one moment Lindsay almost felt sorry for him, but she knew she had to make him understand. Taking a deep breath, she said, 'I'm sorry you've come all this way for nothing, Andrew—'

'It needn't be that way.' He persisted.

'But, you see,' she carried on, not giving him a chance to say any more, 'there's something you don't know…'

'Are you all right, Lindsay?' It was some time later and Henry had come into the study after seeing Andrew out to his car.

'Yes,' she replied with a sigh, 'I'm OK.' She felt exhausted really but at the same time curiously satisfied, as if some unfinished issue had finally been resolved.

'He's gone,' said Henry.

'I hope he doesn't intend driving all the way back to London tonight,' Lindsay replied wearily.

'No, I persuaded him to check into a hotel I know in Llangollen.'

'I told him it was over before I came here, Henry.'

'Yes, I know you did. It seems he just wasn't prepared to take no for an answer.'

'I think it was more a case of injured pride. I doubt if Andrew Barlow has ever been turned down before in his life. But at least it's proved one thing to me.'

'Oh?' said Henry, 'and what's that?'

'I really am over him,' Lindsay replied. 'When I first came here, although I knew in my heart that the relationship was over, I wasn't sure I was over *him*, if you know what I mean.'

'Ah,' said Henry knowingly. 'In my experience, the only cure for a broken heart is to love again.'

Lindsay smiled and turned towards the door. 'Where's Aidan, Henry?' she asked.

'He's gone home, Lindsay. He left as soon as he knew who your visitor was. I told him I would take you home.'

'Thank you, Henry. But I don't want to go the flat.'

'Now, how did I know that was what you were going to say? Come on, we'll go now. Megan will be all right for a while.'

Together they left the house, and almost in silence Henry drove her to Aidan's cottage. When they were nearly there he threw Lindsay a sidelong glance. 'I never did get around to asking Aidan the purpose of your visit. Somehow I can't imagine it was simply to tell me that Clarrie had given birth to a daughter, delightful as that news is, of course.'

'You're quite right, Henry—that wasn't the reason for our visit,' Lindsay replied.

'So are you going to tell me what it was?'

She took a deep breath. 'Yes, all right,' she said at last. 'Although somehow I have the feeling you know anyway...'

\* \* \*

Henry dropped her off on the road above the cottage, at the top of the steps. It was twilight by this time and in spite of a single lamp that burned on the wall she had to take care of the steep steps so as not to lose her footing. By the time she reached the door the dogs had heralded her approach. She lifted her hand and knocked. The dogs continued to bark from inside the cottage and for a moment she thought Aidan wasn't there. It was true that his Land Rover hadn't been up on the road but she knew that at night he usually parked it in the lane at the front of the cottage.

He had to be there, she thought in growing desperation. She had to see him. Now, tonight, she had to see him. God only knew what he was thinking, with Andrew turning up like that out of the blue. Why, he might even now be thinking that she was preparing to return to London and pick up the threads of her old life. Frantically she hammered again on the door and inside the dogs almost went demented.

Lindsay had just about given up, convinced that he wasn't there, when she heard a sound behind her and she spun round. He was walking towards her up through the tangled darkness of the garden.

'Aidan. Oh, Aidan,' she gasped in relief. 'I didn't think you were here.'

'I went for a walk.' He spoke abruptly, before growling a single command to the dogs who instantly fell silent.

'Without the dogs?' she said incredulously. It was unheard of for Aidan to go anywhere, especially for a walk, without his dogs.

'I needed some space to think.' He stopped in front of her, his gaze meeting hers in the eerie light. A moth fluttered above their heads and darted around the lamp on the wall.

'Did you come to any conclusions?' she asked softly.

'I didn't know what to think.' His voice was hoarse, gruff.

'And now?'

'I still don't know what to think.' He inhaled sharply. 'If you've come to tell me you've changed your mind, can we get it over quickly?'

'Oh, Aidan. Is that what you think?' Reaching out her hand, she touched his cheek. It felt rough, the stubble reminding her that it had been a long day.

'I told you, I don't know what to think.' Grasping Lindsay's hand in his, he held it against his face, the gesture somehow both tender and desperate.

'But I told you before that that particular relationship was over.'

'You also said you weren't sure you were over him...so when he turns up here how am I to know what to think?'

'But when I told you that, it was before...before you and I...'

'What are you saying, Lindsay?' He gripped both her hands tightly.

'That I love you, Aidan. I love you and I want to be with you. I thought I was in love with Andrew once, but he killed that love and since I've met you I've realised the love I feel for you is so much more.'

He continued to stare at her in the half-light then with a sort of groan of desperation he stepped forward and roughly pulled her into his arms.

In the moment before his mouth covered hers she told herself that this was truly where she was meant to be, and the shaft of desire deep inside, which was now becoming very familiar, simply confirmed that fact.

When at last they drew apart it was Lindsay who spoke first. 'Henry knows about us, Aidan.' Her voice sounded shaky.

'Yes, I rather gathered he knew by his manner towards me when you went in with…with him…' Aidan obviously had difficulty in saying Andrew's name.

'His manner?'

'Yes, sort of fatherly.'

'Bless him.' Lindsay smiled in the darkness. 'I got the impression he's known all along. In fact, I would go so far as to say that it was what he and Megan were hoping might happen. I dare say they're celebrating at this very moment.'

'So you don't think there'll be any objections about me being your trainer?'

'I asked him that and he said, no, not as far as he was concerned, and as long as we carried out our duties properly he couldn't see that anyone else would be bothered either.'

'We'll do that, won't we?' Drawing her into his arms again, he kissed her forehead, then the tip of her nose.

'But of course.'

They were silent for a moment, safe in each other's arms. The only sounds around them were those of a summer's night—small scurryings in the undergrowth and the distant call of an owl. For Lindsay it seemed a million miles away from her old life in London, but at the same time it felt utterly right. She knew she'd never been so sure about anything or anyone in her whole life as she was at this moment, in this garden, with this man.

'I don't know why we're standing out here,' said Aidan at last.

'I think it's rather romantic,' Lindsay replied softly.

'Maybe,' Aidan agreed. 'But I can think of somewhere even more romantic.' Turning, he opened the cottage door. Taking Lindsay's hand, he drew her inside, before closing the door firmly behind them.

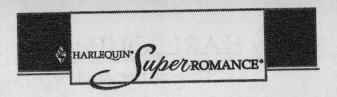

HARLEQUIN® *Super*ROMANCE®

# ...there's more to the story!

Superromance.
A *big* satisfying read about unforgettable
characters. Each month we offer *six* very different
stories that range from family drama to adventure
and mystery, from highly emotional stories to
romantic comedies—and much more! Stories
about people you'll believe in and care about.
Stories too compelling to put down....

Our authors are among today's *best* romance
writers. You'll find familiar names and talented
newcomers. Many of them are award winners—
and you'll see why!

If you want the biggest and best
in romance fiction, you'll get it
from Superromance!

## Emotional, Exciting, Unexpected...

HARLEQUIN®
*M*akes any time special ®

# HARLEQUIN®
## *Makes any time special* ®

**Upbeat, All-American Romances**

HARLEQUIN®
**Duets**™

**Romantic Comedy**

**Historical, Romantic Adventure**

HARLEQUIN®
# INTRIGUE
**Romantic Suspense**

*Harlequin Romance*®
**Capturing the World You Dream Of**

HARLEQUIN® *Presents*

**Seduction and passion guaranteed**

HARLEQUIN® *Super* ROMANCE®

**Emotional, Exciting, Unexpected**

HARLEQUIN®
*Temptation*

**Sassy, Sexy, Seductive!**

HDIR1

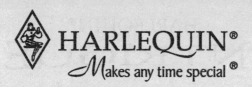

# HARLEQUIN®
*Makes any time special* ®

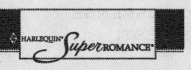

# HARLEQUIN®
# INTRIGUE

## WE'LL LEAVE YOU BREATHLESS!

If you've been looking for thrilling tales of
contemporary passion and sensuous love stories
with taut, edge-of-the-seat suspense—then
you'll love Harlequin Intrigue!

Every month, you'll meet four new heroes
who are guaranteed to make your spine tingle
and your pulse pound. With them you'll enter
into the exciting world of Harlequin Intrigue—
where your life is on the line
and so is your heart!

## THAT'S INTRIGUE—
## ROMANTIC SUSPENSE
## AT ITS BEST!

# HARLEQUIN®
*Makes any time special* ®

# Medical Romance™

# COMING NEXT MONTH

### #11 RESCUING DR. RYAN by Caroline Anderson

Dr. Will Ryan was supposed to be training the beautiful Dr. Lucie Compton, but having injured himself in a fall he now finds that he is totally dependent upon her for help. Forced into constant contact, they drive each other crazy—in more ways than one....

### #12 FOUND: ONE HUSBAND by Meredith Webber

Out in the Australian rain forest an injured man literally dropped into nurse Sam Abbott's life. Getting him back to safety was one problem, dealing with his amnesia was going to present many more. All he could remember was some medical knowledge. Was he a doctor? All Sam knew was that her attraction for this intriguing stranger with a wedding ring was about to lead her into unknown territory!

### #13 A WIFE FOR DR. CUNNINGHAM by Maggie Kingsley

Junior doctor Hannah Blake knows she can prove her value to the emergency unit team at St. Stephen's, but her relationship with workaholic Dr. Robert Cunningham could be her undoing. He might accept her as a colleague, even as a lover—but will he ever see her as a wife?

### #14 RELUCTANT PARTNERS by Margaret Barker

When the man that Dr. Jane Crowther believes stood her up all those years ago joins her practice, she is determined not to fall for his charms again. But G.P. Richard has no recollection of their date and sets about trying to unravel the past and to win Jane's love....

MEDICALCNM0401